x   c.1

Lampman, Evelyn
Sibley

Squaw man's son

DATE			
JUL 6 - '79			
APR 7 '80			
MAY 7 '85			
SEP 1 9 '86			
OCT 7 '90			
NOV - 7 '9			
NOV 2 9 2001			
MAR 07 '12			

Other Books by Evelyn Sibley Lampman

White Captives
Rattlesnake Cave
Go Up the Road
The Potlatch Family
Bargain Bride

(MARGARET K. MC ELDERRY BOOKS)

Squaw
Man's
Son

Squaw Man's Son

Evelyn Sibley Lampman

A MARGARET K. MCELDERRY BOOK

Atheneum   1978   New York

Map by Anita Karl

Library of Congress Cataloging in Publication Data
Lampman, Evelyn Sibley.
Squaw Man's Son.
"A Margaret K. McElderry book."
SUMMARY: Because he is part Indian and part white
a thirteen-year-old boy begins to realize
he doesn't fit into either culture.
[1. Modoc Indians—Fiction. 2. Indians of North
America—Fiction] I. Title.
PZ7.L185Sq   [Fic]   77–17503
ISBN 0–689–50102–1

Published simultaneously in Canada by
McClelland & Stewart, Ltd.
Manufactured in the United States of America by
Fairfield Graphics, Fairfield, Pennsylvania
Designed by Marjorie Zaum
First Printing February 1978
Second Printing December 1978
X
c.1

Squaw
Man's
Son

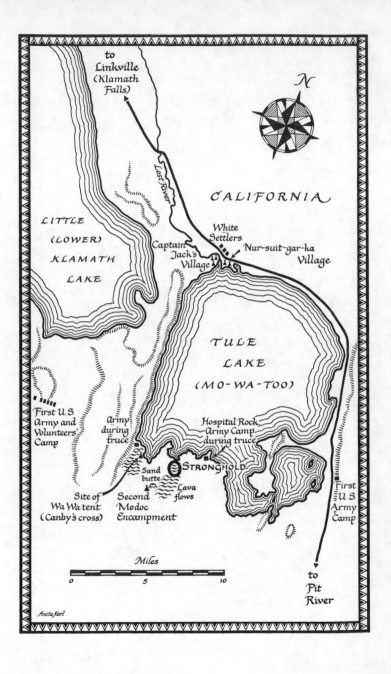

Chapter One

"IT'S MIGHTY TEMPTIN'. MIGHTY TEMPTIN'!" PA HAD been trying to keep his voice low, but this time he forgot and the final words came booming through the rough boards of the partition.

Billy, who had been sent to the back of the livery stable to mend a broken harness, tilted his head to hear better.

" 'T'ain't like you're all alone. You got the boy." That was Mayor Goodrich. He had a high-pitched voice that carried, and Billy had been able to catch most of his words. The trouble was the mayor hadn't said much. It was Sheriff McVey who had done most of the talking and his low rumble was hard to hear.

"*Sh,*" warned Pa, as though reminded that his son was only a few feet away. "He's got Injun ears, that one."

"Still, he don't show it too much," said the mayor. "And that's good. He could pass if the light wasn't too bright. And if you cut his hair."

"Billy!" shouted Pa. "C'mere."

Billy put down the bits of leather and crossed the splintery floor into the outer room.

Of the three men Pa was far and away the biggest. He had wide shoulders from which grew massive arms and hands. Red tangled curls covered his large head and the beard that almost concealed his face was red and curly too. Pa's temper was short and when he was riled his brows dropped low over his eyes. That was the danger sign, and when it happened Billy's mother had taught him to be very quiet and to hurry and do whatever Pa wanted. She was more than a little afraid of Pa, although Billy had never seen him beat her, and despite daily threats he only whipped his son when Billy was really bad. Not that he had been bad very often. Usually when Pa was home he was sleeping or glumly eating his meals without unnecessary talk, occasionally giving brief loud-voiced orders about what he wanted done. He spent more time in town than he did at home, and both Billy and his mother were glad of that.

Pa's callers were practically strangers to Billy, and until this morning he could not recall either of them setting foot in the livery stable. Nobody came to the stable to visit, only on business, and then they didn't linger. Somehow, Billy had got the idea that Pa didn't have many friends in town. Today was the exception. Billy knew who they were, of course, and from afar he had admired the mayor's silk hat, tall and shiny as a black pebble in the bottom of a lake. And he also admired the silver star which decorated the sheriff's

4

plaid wool shirt. Although they often passed him in the street, they had never spoken to him, and the only time they ever looked at him was when Pa wasn't around. Then their eyes dwelt on him curiously, as they might on a wild bear chained in captivity.

They were staring openly now, even though Pa was sitting there.

"He's going to be a big 'un," observed Sheriff McVey. "Maybe up to your size, Mose. How old is he now?"

Pa's forehead wrinkled as he considered the matter. He could have asked, but he didn't, so Billy didn't tell him that he was thirteen.

"Must be 'bout twelve," said Pa finally. "He was slow starting to grow. Many's the time I figured he'd turn out a runt. Then all of a sudden, he started growing. He's strong for his age, too. He can heft a bale of hay near as good as me."

Every bit as well as you, thought Billy, but he didn't say it. Once he himself had despaired of growing tall and strong. It seemed that he was thin and spindling for a long time. Of course, being small had its compensations. If he had been big enough to help out in the stable Pa would never have let him and his mother spend that time on the Lost River with her people, for instance. They had only gone once, and their stay had been brief. Pa had come after them in a week because he was tired of doing his own cooking and washing.

Billy knew it would never happen again. A year ago he had started to grow. During a single summer his arms and legs had lengthened like the sprouts of willow in the spring. He could carry heavy buckets filled with water as easily as his mother.

One day Pa said, "Reckon you're big enough to start helping out in the stable."

"Reckon so," Billy agreed, and the next morning he went to work with Pa. He had been there every day since.

"You figure he's smart enough to take over should you have to be gone a day or so?" asked Sheriff McVey thoughtfully.

"Oh, he's smart," agreed Pa. "Smart as a fox. He can rub down a horse slicker'n a hazel whistle. I even learned him how to make change for a dollar." Billy could hardly believe he was hearing right. Pa had never praised anything he had done before. But with his next words, Pa became his usual self. "He knows I'd whip him bloody if he didn't do right."

"Well then?" prompted Mayor Goodrich in his high, piping voice.

Pa glowered at the mayor.

"Billy, you go home and get your dinner," he ordered. "You can eat first today. I ain't hungry yet."

"It's early. Ma won't have it ready." Billy spoke without thinking.

"Then tell her to fix it. And stay there till she does."

Billy fled before the anger he could see building in his father's face.

Mose Morrison's livery stable was on one end of the main street of Linkville. The little Oregon town, close to the northern California border, did not encompass many blocks, nor were the buildings pretentious, but to Billy, who had seen no others, they seemed very grand. There was a general store, which sold everything from miners' picks and farmers' plows to ladies' dress goods and grocery supplies like sugar and coffee.

There was a butcher shop, a barber shop, a harness shop, a self-styled hotel and two saloons. There was the tiny office which sold stage coach tickets and handled freight orders, and a laundry run by two Chinese. It was a flourishing town, with steep hills rising at its back, and in summer all these establishments were enveloped in a cloud of saffron dust, constantly stirred up by the horses and wagons using the street between. In winter there was no dust, but the street became a rutty trail of brown, sticky mud that sucked at the horses' hooves and threatened to mire down every wagon.

Notwithstanding the mud, Billy walked in the street itself. Experience had taught him that if he tried to make his way on the planks thrown down in front of the business houses, someone would force him off. Whites did not give way to boys who were half Indian.

As he passed the first saloon, he heard a sound that was curiously out of place. It was the raucus "*Kwa, kwa, kwa*" of a wild duck. Nearby Klamath Lake and Tule Lake, where the Modoc Indians once made their home, abounded in ducks of many varieties. There were also pelicans and herons, cormorants and so many different kinds of water fowl Billy could not name them all. But ducks did not leave the wilds for the busy center of town. This was a different kind of animal.

He stopped, feeling his feet settle more deeply in the mud, and turned toward the direction from which the sound had come.

Standing below the overhanging roof of the saloon was a boy close to his own age. His clothes were a curious collection of castoffs, all ragged, and all designed for much larger men. Stringy blond hair hung below the battered felt hat on his head, and the dirt on his thin, pinched face was visible even from this distance.

"*Kwa, kwa, kwa!*" Billy returned the signal.

"Your pa let you off early?" called the boy. "You through for the day? I got one more saloon to sweep out, then I got nothing to do. We could go down to the lake. Maybe fish a little."

"I can't, Bud." Billy stepped aside for a creaking wagon to jolt past. "Pa sent me home to eat dinner. Then I got to go back."

"But it's no more than ten o'clock," protested Bud. "You pa's off his rocker."

"He just wanted to get rid of me," Billy explained. "He's talking to the mayor and Sheriff McVey. He didn't want me to hear."

"What about?"

"I don't know." Billy shrugged. "But it's got something to do with me."

"I'll smell around and see if I can find out anything," promised Bud. "Somebody's sure to let something drop."

"You do that." Billy grinned warmly at his friend. His only friend, he reminded himself as he started on.

Bud was an orphan who, for years, had lived by his own efforts, sleeping wherever he could, making a little money cleaning saloons, and surviving on other people's castoffs. No one knew who his parents were and Bud didn't either. He had meandered up the coast from San Francisco by slow stages, stopping awhile in towns along the way. Billy hoped he would stay in Linkville. It was nice to have a friend.

As he came within sight of his home on the edge of town he was surprised to see two horses standing in the yard. Ponies, he corrected himself as he drew closer. Indian ponies. His mother had visitors. It was a foolish thing for her to do. What if Pa came home unexpectedly and found them there? Pa didn't allow Indians in his house.

Once, several months before when the Modocs had been forced to move from their old home on Lost River and Tule Lake and onto the Klamath Reservation, Billy's grandfather, Deaf Tom, had called upon his daughter. Pa had found him there and literally thrown the old man down the porch steps. He had never come again, nor had any of the tribe. Billy knew that his mother would have liked to visit them, but Pa wouldn't hear of that, either. It made his heart sad to see his mother's wistful face and know that she was thinking of her people, now so close but still denied to her.

As he crossed the yard he could see the pony tracks quite clearly in the mud. Before he left, he must make sure to erase them. Pa was no fool. He would see unshod hoofmarks, and it would cause trouble.

There were two Indians sitting on the floor beside the open fire place. Each had a mug of coffee in his hands, and after her first startled gasp at the opening of the door his mother relaxed and the smile returned to her face. It was the first time Billy had seen her smile for a long time.

Even though it had been several years since his visit to the Lost River, Billy recognized both the men. One was Kientepoos, now known as Captain Jack, chief of the Modocs, while the other was called Bogus Charley.

Captain Jack was still young in years, nor had he been chief for very long. When the old chief Schonchin grew too feeble to lead, Jack had been chosen to take his place because he was deemed wisest in the tribe.

Even those who grumbled that Jack was too cautious never questioned his wisdom. Many whites, in the settlement of Yreka, called him friend, and after pondering their advice Jack maintained that the whites and Modocs must live together in peace. When the young, hot-blooded braves called for war, it was Jack who held them back.

"They are too many for us," he insisted. "We have few guns, while they have thousands. It is better to give up a little of our land than to die and lose it all."

One day the Peace Commissioner of the whites crossed the mountains and called the Modocs together for a talk. He said more white settlers were coming to this land. They would need more space. Even now the cattle of the settlers grazed farther than ever into Modoc territory. The whites were turning over the soil with their plows, breaking down berry bushes and spoiling the spots where Modoc women had always gone to dig roots. If these settlers were killed, even more would come to take their places and with them soldiers with guns. Soon every Modoc would die, even to the smallest child.

Deaf Tom, who had had time to tell Billy and his mother of this meeting before Pa threw him out, had shaken his head sadly at the remembrance. He was an old man, and changes were hard for him to endure.

The white man from across the mountains wanted the Modocs to move to Klamath land, now known as a reservation. There no one would die. They could live safely as they had before, and no one would molest them. Klamath land was not unlike their own. It had lakes and rivers, the same roots and berries grew there, the same game was abundant. The Klamaths would welcome them as brothers.

Captain Jack and John Schonchin, younger brother of the old chief and now sub-chief of the tribe, listened carefully as the interpreter gave them the man's words. After much talk, they persuaded the Modocs to go. It was the only safe thing to do.

Soon eight big wagons, drawn by mules, came to transport all their belongings to the new reservation. Women and children sat in the wagon, and the men rode their ponies. They took possession of a point of land above the lake, and Allen David, chief of the Klamaths, and Captain Jack covered an axe with boughs of pine, symbol that their ancient enmity was ended. Then many presents were given by the Indian agent to both tribes, blankets, shirts, cloth for men's trousers and women's dresses, thread, needles and buttons to use in the making. When they saw the presents, even the warriors who had grumbled agreed that Captain Jack was wise. They mingled freely with the Klamaths at the feast that followed and spoke of the good life they would share together.

Billy, too, thought that Captain Jack had been wise. Before, there had been much killing, Indians as well as whites, but all that was ended. There was peace and life for all, not death. Now, as he looked into those steady black eyes regarding him so carefully, the round, brown face with its firm, well-shaped mouth, he was proud to remember that this man was a kinsman of his mother.

Jack wore a striped cotton shirt and a pair of baggy, homemade woolen trousers. His hair was parted in the middle and cut short just below his ears. The hand which he extended was hard and calloused from heavy work, but the clasp was firm and warm from the heat of the fire.

"Do you remember my son, Billy Morrison?" asked Mother. She spoke fondly and in the Modoc tongue.

"He has no Modoc name?" asked Captain Jack severely.

"I gave him none." Mother's face flushed with embarrassment. "My man did not wish it."

"Why should he need one?" asked the man sitting opposite, and Billy turned to him gratefully. Captain Jack's words had been like the bite of a hornet, and for the first time he wished his mother had given him an Indian name, even in secret.

"No one needs an Indian name any more," continued the man. "We have all taken new names from the whites. Look at me. I've even forgotten what my old name was."

Billy remembered Bogus Charley well. Unlike Captain Jack's, his eyes were small and the skin around them was crinkled with constant laughter. He had full lips and a nose with spreading nostrils. He was always telling jokes, and children followed him around waiting to hear what he would say next.

"Where is your father?" Billy's mother asked nervously.

When Billy told her he was to eat first today, she relaxed and refilled her guests' mugs with coffee, adding great spoonsful of sugar to each.

"I am glad that you have come," said Billy courteously. Even though he had no Indian name he knew the Modoc tongue. Since he was small his mother had spoken it to him when they were alone. They always changed to English whenever Pa arrived. "My mother has been thirsting for news."

"I promised your grandfather I would speak with

her," said Captain Jack. "He wanted her to know that we are moving."

"You're going back to the Lost River?"

"No, but we will leave Modoc Point and make a new camp a day's ride upriver," Captain Jack told him.

"But why?" It was rude to question a chief, but the words were out before Billy remembered.

"Because of those rascally Klamaths." Bogus Charley was the one who answered. The laughter in his eyes dissolved into hatred. "Our people had been cutting railroad ties. The agent pays for each one that is cut. The Modocs worked hard for many days. Nine hundred was the count. Do you know how big a stack that makes?"

Billy shook his head.

"It's halfway to the sky." Bogus Charley paused to make sure the boy understood. "Higher maybe. If you stacked them end to end they could hold the sky up."

Billy blinked. He couldn't imagine so great a pile of cut timber.

"Wouldn't the agent buy them after all?" he asked.

"How could he?" demanded Bogus Charley scornfully. "The thieving Klamaths came at night with wagons and hauled them all away. They said the trees were theirs. They had grown on their land and they belonged to them."

"The agent knows about it now," Captain Jack reminded him calmly. "You told him today."

"Then he will make the Klamaths give them back," said Billy. It would have to be so. Hadn't the Klamaths promised to live as brothers?

"No," denied Bogus Charley angrily. "He said the

ties are gone now and we must forget them."

"But he also said that he would speak with the Klamaths," Captain Jack reminded him. "He said it would not happen again. He said we must move upriver where we are out of sight. It is the young Klamaths who stir up trouble, and if they do not see us every day they will soon forget we are here. The agent does not want trouble. Neither do I." He stood up and reached for a blanket that had been warming before the fire. Folded around his shoulders, it was his outer wrap. "We must return to our people. But I will tell Deaf Tom that I have seen his daughter, and that his grandson will soon be as tall as a young pine tree in the clearing."

After they had gone, his mother washed and dried the coffee mugs used by their guests and put them away. Since he wasn't hungry, Billy refused dinner. He was thinking of the things Bogus Charley had told them.

"It was very wrong for the Klamaths to steal the railroad ties," he said finally. "They should be punished."

"What can you expect?" asked his mother. "When I was young, our elders never let us go out by ourselves. There was danger that a Klamath hunting party would steal children who were unprotected. They sold them as slaves each year at Wishram. If they stole children why wouldn't they steal fallen trees?"

"But they promised to live as brothers," protested Billy.

"The land is theirs. It isn't ours," his mother said thoughtfully. "Perhaps there is something in what they said. Our land is in the south. Our people should return there."

"But they can't," Billy reminded her. "The Modocs have to live here, on the reservation. They share it with the Klamaths. The agent should have made them return the ties. He's the one to blame."

His mother glanced at him briefly, but did not answer. There was no need. Billy knew what she was thinking. The ways of the white man were beyond understanding. But they were strong, and to live, the Indians must obey.

Billy remained home about an hour then, stuffing a piece of biscuit in his pocket, he returned to the livery stable.

Mayor Goodrich and Sheriff McVey were gone when he arrived, and Pa was alone. He looked up briefly but did not speak, and Billy returned to his harness mending.

At noon Pa went home for dinner, and no sooner had he gone than there was the *"Kwa, kwa, kwa!"* of the female duck from the enclosed lot behind the barn. Billy hurried to unbar the heavy back doors which were always kept locked.

"Well, I found out something," announced Bud, stepping inside. He removed his misshapen felt hat and shook it free from the cold rain that was beginning to fall. His pinched face looked more like a little old man's than a boy's.

"So soon?" Billy was astonished. Usually it took Bud longer than this to put together the snatches of conversation he overheard while he was sweeping.

"It's all over town," explained his friend. "Everybody's talking about it. Sheriff McVey wants your pa to be his deputy."

"Pa? Deputy Sheriff?" Billy could hardly believe it. It was a great honor and not bestowed on everyone.

Of course, Pa would be a good one. He was big and short-tempered. Men would think twice before messing with Pa. Billy had never seen him shoot a gun, but he didn't doubt for a minute that Pa could do it.

"The only trouble is that he's"—Bud hesitated delicately before coming out with the word—"a squaw man. Most folks in Linkville don't hold with that."

Billy nodded soberly. He thought of his mother, gentle, quiet, hard-working, uncomplaining. And he remembered the white women for whom he had to step off the plank walk. Some of them were loud. Others bossy. After a disdainful sniff, they all turned their eyes away from Billy and held their skirts so they would not brush against him. Yes, his mother was very different from those white women.

"But things have got so bad around here, they got to do something," continued Bud. "The Sheriff's a good enough man and everybody likes him, but he don't scare nobody. That's why they had a meeting and decided to put it up to your pa. If he'll get rid of his squaw, he can have the job. Maybe even be full sheriff next time."

"Get rid of my mother!" Billy's stomach seemed to rise and push against his chest. He felt cold, as though a blast of air from the snow mountain was all around him.

"I don't know what he said to them," admitted Bud. "Only what they said to him. But if I had a nice wife like your ma I wouldn't get rid of her no matter what anybody said. I'd tell them all to jump in Klamath Lake. Or else I'd throw them in myself."

"I'm going home," said Billy. "Stay and watch the stable for me."

Before Bud could answer, he was out the door and running down the street. He had not stopped for a coat, but he didn't notice the rain which soon soaked through his shirt. He automatically dodged wagons and riders on horseback, and when some of the drivers yelled at him angrily, he did not hear. His only concern was for his mother. Would Pa kill her? Was that what the men meant by getting rid of her? It was no sin to kill an Indian. It happened all the time.

But when he reached home and threw open the door, his mother was alive. She was making up a bundle of small things, tying them in a blanket, while his father sat at the table spooning up great bites of the elk stew she had prepared.

"Why ain't you at the stable?" he shouted angrily. "I left you in charge."

"Because I heard—I know . . ." He stumbled over his words and felt awkward and ashamed. He should have known Pa wouldn't do anything really bad. "Bud's watching the stable for me."

"You heard that I'm going to be deputy sheriff and wear a star," said Pa. He sat up proudly. "Well, it's true. And maybe it's just as well you come. You can say good-bye to your ma now that you're here."

"I go to my own people," said his mother. Usually she never spoke in Modoc in front of Pa, but today she did. It was as though she was no longer afraid.

"She's going back to her own tribe." Since Pa did not speak the language, he didn't know that he was repeating her words. "Getting her stuff together right now."

"Then I will get mine," said Billy promptly.

"Hold your horses," shouted Pa. "You're not going no place. I already told your ma, and now I'll tell you. You're staying with me. You're my son, and I need you."

"You need me to run the livery barn while you're off being sheriff," accused Billy bravely. If Pa wanted to whip him with the leather strap, he could. But he would have his say. "Well, I'm half Indian. Long as I'm here people will remember you used to have a squaw for a wife. I better get out too."

"No such thing. It's all arranged. And keep a civil tongue in your head." The heavy brows dropped even closer to Pa's eyes and the strip of forehead underneath the tangled red curls flushed with anger. "You'll do like I say, or I'll thrash you bloody."

"You must stay here," said his mother gently. "He is your father and your place is with him. You are half white and must live as a white. I am Modoc, and it is right that I go with my people. My heart is glad to leave this place, but inside I will cry each day because I must leave you behind."

"Do you want me to stay, my mother?" asked Billy. He couldn't believe she would say yes. All those early years before he grew tall, they had been so close, just the two of them against everyone else.

"It is not what I want. It is the white man's way, and we cannot go against that," she reminded him. "A son belongs to his father."

She tied the four corners of the blanket holding her possessions and folded a second one around herself for a wrap. For a moment she pressed her cheek against Billy's. Then she opened the door and when she closed it from the outside he knew that she was gone forever.

18

Chapter Two

"I BETTER GO BACK," SAID BILLY. HIS THROAT HAD grown so dry that his voice sounded hoarse and grating. "I told Bud to watch things while I was gone."

If he left right now he could overtake his mother. She didn't understand. "A boy belongs to his father," she had said. "It is the white man's way." But Billy was only half white. He had as much right to go with her as he did to stay here.

"I'm done eating. We'll both go back," said Pa. He pushed back his chair and stood up. "That was right smart of you to get Bud to stay while you was gone. Not that I'd want you to make a practice of it, but just this once."

Billy looked at his father in amazement. He had expected anger, not approval, for leaving Bud in charge. It was the second time that day Pa had paid him a compliment.

There was no sign of his mother when they came outside. The rain had become a heavy drizzle. It clouded the distance like thick fog. Billy stared up the road in the direction she must have taken, but she was out of sight. He could picture her, though, wrapped in one blanket with the second blanket-bundle across her shoulder. She would be striding along, headed for the reservation. She was glad to leave Linkville, but he had felt tears on her cheek when she told him good-bye. He knew they were for him.

"You promise to pay Bud for watching things?" asked Pa as they headed in the opposite direction.

"No," said Billy. "He'll do it because he's my friend."

Pa grunted, but said nothing. They plodded on silently through the rain, and Billy wished he had the courage to break away and run after his mother. But he didn't. He was too afraid of Pa.

When they reached the business district, Billy continued on in the road but Pa called him over to the side.

"From now on, you'll walk on the planks like everybody else," he ordered. "No son of mine's going to be kicked off into the mud."

Billy could have told him it wouldn't work, but he held his tongue. There was no sense arguing with Pa. He'd have to see the way things were for himself. He stepped onto the plank and followed closely in his father's footsteps.

Several times they met acquaintances and Pa greeted them, holding firm on the slippery board. Confronted by his great bulk it was the others who made way while Pa proceeded on. Billy, too, walking as close to Pa as he dared, stayed on the plank. He didn't look at those waiting in the mud, but he knew they were glaring at him resentfully, and it made him uncomfortable. He'd much rather have been walking in the road. He didn't know what had come over Pa. He'd never acted this way before.

His behavior was even odder when they reached the livery stable.

"For your trouble," he said, tossing a couple of copper pennies to the wide-eyed Bud, who looked as though he were ready to dash through the door. Pa had never liked Bud. He called him "trash" and names that were even worse. "Anybody come in?"

Bud shook his head, fumbling for the pennies on the floor.

"Then you can handle things a mite longer." Pa's tone was almost genial. "Me and my son got a little errand."

Bud nodded mutely. His eyes sought Billy's, but Billy was as much at a loss as he. This was a side of Pa he had never seen.

Once again the two went out into the rain. Pa led the way back down the street. This time he did step off the plank long enough for a lady to pass.

She was a stranger to Billy, and undoubtedly to Pa as well, for he called her "ma'am" and not by name as he would have done to a citizen of Linkville. He doffed his hat with a courtly bow, which she returned with a brief nod of her head before continuing on. She did not hold her skirts away from Billy's contaminating touch. In fact, she was so busy looking at Pa that she scarcely spared Billy a glance, but he stared at her.

She was tall for a woman and very thin. He could tell that even though most of her figure was protected by an enveloping shawl. He couldn't see much of her hair beneath the damp, wilting bonnet, and he had only a glimpse of her face before she hurried by. But he could tell that she wasn't too young, maybe his mother's age, and that her eyes were quick and darting.

Pa's errand was in Pete Barnes's barber shop. He opened the door, after glancing over his shoulder to make sure his son was following.

It was warm inside. The heat came from a small iron stove that was glowing red on the sides. Billy hadn't seen many iron stoves up close, so he examined it carefully before his eyes took in the other details of the single room.

There was a bench under the rain-spotted window where people could sit, and a couple of extra straight-backed chairs. A row of shelves had been nailed against one wall to hold bottles and a long line of shaving mugs, each inscribed with somebody's name. At least, Billy guessed they were people's names. He had never learned to read, but Pa had such a mug, filled with soap and holding a handled brush, with similar markings on it. Once when he was in an expansive mood, he had told Billy that the strange marks were his name, Moses Morrison. They meant that the mug belonged to him and no one else dared touch it. Terrible things would happen to anyone who did.

In the center of the room was a chair with arms. It was higher than the others, for each leg was standing on a block of wood. It sat all alone, and until they arrived Pete Barnes had been occupying it. Now he got up and came forward to greet Pa.

"Howdy, Mose. Hear congratulations are in order."

"Just doing my civic duty," said Pa. "Seen a strange lady just now, Pete. New family moved in?"

"That's right. Name's Green. Bought the Tolliver place. Haven't heard yet what they paid for it but Luke Tolliver's grinning like a cat that ate the canary, so I reckon he got a fair price. Hear there's three of them. Mr. and Mrs. and Mr.'s sister. Guess she's an old maid, leastwise that's what Ed Quincy says. He was there when Mrs. and the sister come in on the stage. Says the sister's got a tongue sharp as a honed razor, yelling at the driver to be careful with that and not to drop this when he unloaded. Had a heap of stuff, too, boxes and even a couple of barrels, along with their satchels."

"Must have been Mrs. that I seen," said Pa, cutting him short. "She was a fine figure of a woman, anyway. Pete, I brung Billy in. Want you should give him a haircut."

"Him?" For the first time the barber looked at Billy and the boy could see the dislike in his eyes. "Ain't his ma going to cut it no more?"

"His ma's gone," Pa told him firmly. "She won't be back. Get into the chair, Billy. Pete's going to cut your hair the way it should be done."

"How you want it cut, Mose?" The barber's voice sounded strange. No longer did his words tumble eagerly. They were slow and a little doubtful.

"You cut my son's hair just the way you cut other boys' hair." Pa sat on the bench, and his eyebrows dropped dangerously low over his eyes.

"Short," said Mr. Barnes promptly. "Mostly when boys get haircuts their mas want it short so they won't have to come back so soon."

"Short then," agreed Pa.

Billy could feel the coolness of the scissors against his neck as the black hair, which his mother had always trimmed to his shoulders, fell away. Mr. Barnes was

23

not as gentle as his mother. He pulled and pushed Billy's head from side to side. Once he felt a prick as though the scissor points had nicked his scalp, and he wondered if it was deliberate. He said nothing, however, nor did the usually talkative Mr. Barnes speak while he was working. Out of the corner of his eye, Billy could see Pa sitting there, observing every move. He didn't blame the barber for going about his business silently.

"There," said Mr. Barnes finally. "All done."

"Tonic," ordered Pa. "You always finish off haircuts with tonic, Pete."

Mr. Barnes took one of the bottles from the shelf, shook several drops on Billy's shorn head, and rubbed them in. Then he combed his hair carefully, making a neat part on the left side.

"Give him a mirror," ordered Pa. "He'll want to see how he looks."

Billy stared into the small hand mirror which was thrust into his hands, and it was like seeing a strange boy. Most of his hair was gone. It lay scattered on the floor beneath Mr. Barnes' feet. There was enough left to brush to each side in front, but the rest was cropped short, an inch from his head. His ears stuck out on either side, and he looked at them wonderingly. Until now he had hardly known he had ears. His whole head felt light, as though it were made of clouds, and the smell of the hair tonic in his nose was sweet and a little sickening.

"Makes a heap of difference," approved Pa. He handed the barber a coin. "C'mon, Billy. Me and you's got to get back to work."

Bud, too, had trouble recognizing Billy when they arrived at the livery stable.

"Your hair!" he gasped. "You look like you been scalped."

"No such thing," denied Pa angrily. "He looks like a white boy now. All white, and not no alley scum neither. Billy's the son of the deputy sheriff of this town, and folks better not forget it, neither."

In the days that followed, Billy could see that his father was taking his new duties very seriously. He spent most of each day in the livery stable, but every night he went back downtown to help Sheriff McVey "keep an eye on things." He bought himself a new wool shirt on which to pin his deputy sheriff's badge and had Pete Barnes cut his hair and trim his beard. But the most remarkable change was in his manner. Although he still glared and expected Billy to jump to obey his orders, there were times when he made an effort to be agreeable. One evening he even explained why he had sent his wife away.

"You see, Billy, there wasn't nothing else I could do," he said. "It ain't that Sally wasn't a good woman, for she was. She worked hard and did her best. It's just that she was the wrong color. And that pulled me down, me and you both. It ain't easy to have folks call you a squaw man. They look down their noses at squaw men around these parts. Then when they told me I could be deputy sheriff if I stopped being one, there was nothing else to do but send Sally packing."

"I'm still her son." Billy looked up from the stew he was eating. It wasn't as good as his mother's stew. He had never paid much attention to the cooking, but now he had to take over that chore along with most of the work at the livery stable. "I'm Indian, too."

"Don't let me hear you say that again. You're my son," roared Pa. "Likely the only one I'll ever have.

Folks will forget about the Injun half, give them enough time. Why with that haircut and the new shirt I bought you, you could pass for all white any day. Lots of whites are dark-complected."

Billy didn't answer, but he knew better. Nobody in Linkville would ever forget. The ladies still sniffed when he passed them on the street. The men were careful to speak to him, particularly when Pa was around, but their eyes remained unfriendly. All the haircuts and fine clothes in the world couldn't change that.

"Tomorrow we're going to church." Pa pushed back his chair, the signal that he had finished eating. "So make sure to wash yourself good and clean. It's been a spell since I was in one, but I recollect that when I was a boy all important people went to church regular. Injuns don't go. So when folks see you there it ought to cinch things for everybody."

He polished his star on his shirt sleeve, put on his coat and departed for the best part of his day, the evening hours when, hopefully, a fight would start in some saloon and the deputy sheriff could bring law and order to Linkville.

Billy hung the stewpot back over the fireplace to rewarm. There wasn't much left. Pa had been extra hungry tonight. A minute or so later he heard the familiar signal from outside."

"*Kwa, kwa, kwa!*"

"Come in, Bud," he called, throwing open the door. "He's gone."

"I know. I seen him on the road." Bud removed his thin, ragged coat, shook it free from the snowflakes that were falling outside, then hung it before the fire.

"He didn't see you?" asked Billy in alarm. "If he

26

did he'd know where you were going."

"I got off in some bushes when I seen somebody coming," said Bud. He unhooked the stewpot from the crane and began ladeling the contents into a bowl. "Didn't leave much tonight," he complained.

"Pa was hungry," Billy told him briefly. He sat down to watch his friend eat.

Every night since his mother had gone, Bud stopped by and finished off what was left of their supper. Billy was glad to have his company. It was lonely night after night while Pa was busy being a deputy sheriff, and Bud was anxious to come. Often this was the only hot meal he had each day, and the warmth of the fire was preferable to a cold shed or someone's hayloft. It must be hard to be an orphan, Billy thought, to have no one who cared about you. Difficult as his own life had been, it was better than Bud's.

"Any news?" he asked, when his friend reluctantly put down the empty bowl.

"Nothing worth telling." Bud poured himself a cup of coffee from the granite pot keeping warm on the hearth. "Folks say your pa's doing a good job. He broke up two fights last night. There'll be even more tonight on account of it's Saturday. He'll be late getting home, so I can stay longer."

"We're going to church tomorrow," Billy told him. For once he had a little news of his own. "Pa says important people always do on Sunday. You ever been to church, Bud?"

"Only when I was in the orphanage. They probably wouldn't let me through the door now," Bud said cheerfully. "It's a wonder they'll let you, being a breed and all."

Billy nodded soberly. Bud was probably right. He had never been to church. Pa had never wanted to attend before, but now that he was a deputy sheriff it must be part of his job. Billy wished that he would be permitted to stay home. He wasn't looking forward to tomorrow at all.

Chapter Three

CHURCH WAS EVEN WORSE THAN HE HAD IMAGINED IT
would be.

It was held in a small frame building off Main
Street. Inside was a single room filled with rows of long
benches. At the opposite end, facing the door, was a
very tall table that couldn't have been very useful for
the top was so small it only held one book. The preacher
stood behind it, facing the people who sat on the
benches.

Pa created something of a stir when he marched
in with Billy at his heels. The room was unheated, but
the first thing Pa did was to remove his coat so everyone could see his shiny deputy sheriff's badge. Billy left
his coat on, and so had most of the people.

Pa picked a bench midway down the aisle, and the
people who were sitting there moved over to make
room. Billy noticed, as he sat down, that they were the

three strangers in town, the Greens, who had bought Luke Tolliver's place.

From his seat on the aisle, he was aware of curious glances thrown in his direction. None of the ladies sniffed, but they might as well have. He could almost feel their resentment at a squaw man and his half-breed son daring to come into this place where only important people were welcome. He hid his cold hands in the sleeves of his coat and tried to sink his neck into the collar.

He was so miserable he hardly listened to the preacher, who seemed to talk on and on about things that were strange to him. It was mostly about some person named Noah who had a great fondness for animals. Billy had never heard of Noah, and he could take animals or leave them alone. Except horses, of course.

Then the preacher stopped talking about Noah and spoke about the people who had remained behind when Noah took the animals on his boat. Apparently they were very wicked and had all drowned. He said the same thing would happen to all the bad people in Linkville if they didn't mend their ways. Billy didn't think that was very likely since everyone he knew could swim. The preacher went on and on about it, and finally Billy stopped listening entirely.

When the preacher finally got tired of talking, the people sang, and the songs were not at all like the ones Billy's mother used to sing to him. He had never heard Pa sing, but he did today and Pa's great booming voice almost drowned out the others. Everyone stood up for the singing, and Billy was glad about that. His foot had gone to sleep, and when he stood he could stamp it around a little until Pa's elbow poked him in the ribs and made him stop.

At last it was over and everyone began to leave.
Billy would have liked to push his way through the
crowd and head for home, but Pa must have guessed
his intention for he held him tightly by one arm. He
had a few words for everyone there.

" 'Morning, Mrs. McVey. Sam. Real nice service,
wasn't it?

"Mrs. Barnes. Pete. You can see that Billy's hair's
growing pretty fast. I'll have to bring him back for another of your haircuts one of these days."

Billy followed along because he had no choice, but
he didn't look up at those who replied. It wasn't until
they were outside and Pa was telling him to shake
hands with the preacher that he dared raise his eyes.

"Didn't know you had a son, Deputy." The
preacher was new to Linkville.

"This is him," said Pa, a little belligerently.
"Name's Billy."

"He doesn't take after you too much." The
preacher stared at the brown skin, the black hair and
eyes, and somewhere in the crowd someone giggled.

"Maybe he's not complexioned like his pa," said a
woman's voice behind them. "But look at the boy's
build. When he gets his growth, they'll be like two peas
in a pod."

"Quite true," agreed the preacher quickly. "I was
just about to remark on that myself. Deputy, have you
made the acquaintance of the Greens? They're new to
our town."

Pa said he hadn't but would admire to do so and
the preacher made the introductions. As the barber had
told them, there were three of them. Mr. Green looked
like what he was, a hard-working farmer. He had the
weathered skin of a man who spent most of his days

31

outside, and hard, calloused hands that were used to heavy labor. His wife was small, with a faded prettiness, and she was shy. She only smiled without saying anything. It was Mr. Green's sister who had said Billy was built like Pa, and she was the same lady they had met on the sidewalk on the trip to the barbershop.

Billy's first hurried impression had been correct. She wasn't exactly young, and she was decidedly thin. Her hair was the shade of wet sand and her eyes were a color somewhere between blue and gray. When she was introduced to Billy she put out her hand like a man, and her bony fingers were neither warm nor cold. Like a snake's skin, he thought for a moment, then put the thought away. The lady couldn't help how her skin felt, and at least she was smiling at him. But it was a smile with her lips, not her eyes.

Pa asked the Greens how they liked it out here, and Mr. Green said fine. The soil was good and he was going to try potatoes next spring. Looked to him like it was good potato growing land.

"But it's a little lonesome for Martha and me," put in Miss Green. "We haven't got acquainted yet."

Pa said yes, he guessed it took a spell to get acquainted, Linkville growing so fast and all.

"Your wife didn't come to service with you this morning?" asked Miss Green.

Pa said he didn't have a wife no more. There was just him and Billy. Miss Green clucked her tongue and said that was sad and the two of them must drive out someday for a good home-cooked meal. Pa thanked her kindly and said anytime, and with that the Greens started for their wagon.

"Now can we go home?" asked Billy in a low voice.

"I'm going downtown and look in at the stable

first. You go on home," said Pa. Then he added thoughtfully. "Build up the fire and start fixing our grub. Maybe if it cooked longer it might be tastier. It's been a mighty long time since I had a good, woman-fixed meal."

The snow began in earnest the next day. It lay thick on the rooftops and fields and covered the plank sidewalk and the muddy expanse on either side. It coated the frozen streets, too, and wagon wheels and horses' hooves pounded it down to a hard surface. The roads outside of town became impassable with drifts so the business at the livery stable was limited to Morrison's own horses and those that boarded there.

The saloon business was brisk, however, since the snow enforced idleness on many. It meant that the deputy sheriff was needed during the day as well as in the evenings. Billy practically ran the stable by himself, and Bud spent most of his time there. They kept a sharp lookout for Pa, and whenever they saw him coming Bud would scoot out the back door and wait until he was gone.

"He might not even care if he found you here," said Billy one day, after Bud had ducked back inside, his head and shoulders coated with white and his teeth chattering.

"Better not take chances," argued Bud. "I'd hate to have him crack my skull the way he does them drunks he throws in jail."

Billy couldn't argue with that. Still, Pa became more unpredicatable every day. No one could foretell his moods. After Ma had gone he had become talkative, as though he were trying to make up for all those years of glowering silence. Now he hardly talked to Billy at all. He didn't yell and bellow as he had before, but it was as though his mind was a long way off.

Every Sunday the two of them went to church, but Billy didn't think that Pa enjoyed it any more than he did. Once he went to sleep in the middle of the preacher's talking, and the man in the bench behind had to shake his shoulder to stop the snoring. The Greens, who lived a mile out of town, were snowbound and had not been back. Their places on the bench were vacant. Nobody else made a move to sit with Pa and Billy.

Finally a warm rain from the south washed the snow away, and Linkville came alive in a sea of mud. For a few days the mud was worse than the snow, but eventually it dried and everything was back to normal. The following Sunday the Greens returned to church, and Billy was glad to see them. At least Mrs. Green had included him in her shy smile of greeting and Miss Green had noticed him enough to see that he had his father's build.

After the service Miss Green repeated her invitation to drive out to their farm for Sunday dinner.

"If the town can spare your services that long, Deputy," she added coyly. "I know how people depend on you."

Billy almost laughed as he saw how Pa swelled up under the compliment. He threw back his shoulders and his chest went out like a pigeon's.

"I calculate Sheriff McVey can handle things," he answered. "Not much doing till after dark anyways."

Billy wasn't sure he was included in the invitation, but Pa took it for granted that Miss Green had meant them both. He hitched a horse to the best single-seated buggy in the stable and climbed into the driver's seat.

"Wonder what we'll have for dinner," he said,

clucking to the horse. "Fried chicken, most likely. When I was a young 'un we always had fried chicken of a Sunday."

It proved to be roast pork instead of chicken, but Billy couldn't remember when he'd had so good a meal. Besides the meat there were potatoes covered with cream gravy, beets in a vinegary sauce, cabbage fried with a little onion, great slices of white bread made by Mrs. Green and quince preserves. There was squash pie which was not brought to the table until all the other things were eaten, and Billy, who had not known about the pie, could only make room for a single piece.

"We got here so late in the year, we didn't have time to do a proper canning when things came in season," explained Miss Green. "Not that we'll starve this winter, but all we'll have till spring is late vegetables. Not even so much as a jar of berry jell or a crock of pickles."

"Now, Etta," said her brother severely. "We can't complain. Folks have been mighty kind selling us from their own supplies."

"I suppose so," she agreed, pouting. "But when we have company it would be nice to set a respectable table."

"It was a fine meal. Don't know when I et a better," Pa assured her quickly. "And me and Billy's mighty beholding."

While the ladies did the dishes, the men sat outside on the single step of the two room cabin, and Billy sat beside them. Mr. Green smoked his pipe and Pa took a great bite from the plug of tobacco he always carried in his back pocket. As the juice accumulated, he spit it out into the dirt beside the step The wind was cold and it would have been more comfortable inside, but Mr. Green said tobacco smoke was not pleasing to the ladies so he always came outside to smoke.

"I've known womenfolk that enjoyed a pipe themselves. Corncobs, mostly," said Pa. "Good go-to-church womenfolks, too, not your saloon girls."

"I know," agreed Mr. Green mildly. "But not my womenfolks. They're too refined for that. Etta, mostly. She's real refined, my sister is."

"I noticed that," agreed Pa.

Billy wondered what the word refined meant. He had never heard it before.

"Back home she was a real leader in the ladies' circle," continued Mr. Green. "When she said a thing was so, it was. Reckon she'll be that way here, too, once she gets her stride."

"You mean the others all did like she said?"

Billy wondered why Pa sounded so interested.

"They sure did," agreed Mr. Green.

At that moment the refined Miss Green opened the door. She was wrapped in a heavy shawl for out of doors, and as her brother raised his eyebrows she laughed a little nervously.

"I was going to impose on the deputy and ask him to look over that new riding mare you bought me, Fred," she explained.

"What for?" asked Mr. Green in surprise. "She's a good mare."

"I'd feel better if the deputy said so," she insisted. "Being as he owns the livery stable, he knows about horses. That is, if he doesn't mind."

"I'd be glad to look her over, ma'am." Pa got to his feet.

Billy stood up, too, but before he could accompany them to the barn Miss Green stopped him.

"Why don't you go in the house and keep Martha company, Billy?" she asked. "Poor thing, she's all alone, what with Fred out here smelling everything up with that awful pipe of his. Martha don't see many people these days, and it'd be a real favor."

Billy doubted that Mrs. Green would welcome his company, but he could hardly refuse. He went back into the house.

Mrs. Green was sitting by the fire, and to his surprise she smiled when she saw him. It was the first time a white woman had ever smiled at him, really smiled with her eyes as well as her mouth. It was almost as though she was prepared to like him for himself.

"You want another piece of pie, Billy?" she asked.

He didn't, but he was afraid to refuse for fear she would think he didn't like it. She brought the pie and he sat, choking it down. It was all they said, but it was nice to sit across from her, smiling shyly as they caught one another's eyes.

Mr. Green finished his pipe and came back inside, but it was some time before Pa and Miss Green returned. When they did they made no explanation for the length of their stay, and Pa was strutting like a single rooster in a hen house.

"Fine little mare," he reported. "You got a good buy, Fred."

Because the days were still short, they left soon afterwards. But the following Sunday they were invited back for dinner. It was much the same except that this time there was fried chicken instead of pork. Afterwards Miss Green and Pa again went to the barn just to see how the mare was getting along.

One of those early days of false spring fell on the

37

following Sunday and Pa invited Miss Green to take dinner with him in the local hotel. Billy was not asked to accompany them, and when Pa announced there was to be a basket social at the church the following week, he was not included in that either.

"He's courting," explained Bud, when Billy spoke of the matter. "Reckon your pa's fixing to get married."

"Pa?" Billy refused to believe it. "Who'd marry him? He's a squaw man."

"But he wouldn't be. Not if he takes himself a white wife. Especially if she's one that gets along with the other ladies in town."

Billy remembered what Mr. Green had said about his sister being a leader. Maybe, when she got acquainted in town, she could make people forget what Pa used to be.

Certainly the two of them were seeing more and more of each other, what with Sunday dinners at the farm and weekly buggy rides as the weather grew warmer. Miss Green seemed to be getting a toehold in the church, too. Pa said she'd joined a quilting bee, whatever that meant, and a missionary society, too. And all the ladies made an effort to have a few words with her after church services.

Pa began sprucing himself up. He had his beard trimmed regularly by Pete Barnes, and Billy had to heat water for him in a tub nearly every week so he could have a bath. He never chewed tobacco on Sunday either, not when there was a chance of Miss Green being around, and once when one of the regular ushers was sick he was even asked to help take up the collection at church.

Even Billy's status had changed a little, and he

knew Miss Green was responsible for that, too. The ladies no longer sniffed and turned their heads away when they saw him. Some of them actually spoke to him. But he could read no friendship in their eyes.

Pa was proud as punch about it though.

"You see, Billy, it's working out. Just like I knowed it would. They've forgotten about Sally. You're a white boy now."

Miss Green's trips to town grew more frequent as spring dissolved into early summer. Every time her brother came into Linkville, she seemed to remember some small item that she needed at the store. Inevitably she would pass the livery stable, and Pa would drop everything to harness up a horse and drive her home. She always claimed it was too much trouble. She could go back with Fred, but Pa wouldn't hear of it.

"It'd be my pleasure," Pa always assured her promptly. "Things is slow right now, and Billy can handle the stable just as good as me."

"I can see he's a handy boy to have around," Miss Green agreed, and her voice had a certain ring of sincerity.

One day when Pa had driven away to return Miss Green and her small purchase to the farm, Billy had a visitor. She was a pleasant-faced, comfortably plump woman in her thirties, wearing a long blue and white calico dress. Strings of beads and shells hung about her neck, and her black hair fell long and straight below her shoulders.

"Kaitch-ka-na!" cried Billy joyfully. He used the Modoc word, meaning Little Chief Woman, although nowdays she was known as Tobey, Tobey Riddle.

Several years ago Tobey had married a white man, Frank Riddle, but for some reason no one ever called

Frank a squaw man. Billy wasn't sure why. Frank wasn't as big or tough as Pa. He had been a miner, but now he had taken land near Yainax where he farmed a little and bred livestock, but he spent most of his time hunting and trapping. He was an unerring shot and people said his rifle had brought down over one hundred bear and seven hundred deer and elk, but Billy didn't think it was fear that kept the whites from calling him a squaw man. It was more likely that Frank didn't care. He and Tobey lived their own lives, sometimes with her people, occasionally with his. They were in constant demand as interpreters, both for Indian agents and the army, and if they considered the occasion serious they gave freely of their services.

"What are you doing here?" Billy demanded.

"I needed salt," she told him, smiling. "And we've been long without coffee. But mostly I am here to see you."

"To see me?"

"I bring you a message from your mother. And she asked that I look into your eyes to see if you are treated well and are happy."

"My father treats me well," he told her honestly. "He does not yell as he once did. We get along. I think he is looking for a wife. A white wife."

"Perhaps that is just as well." Her black eyes probed into his carefully. "Your mother says that you must forget your Modoc blood and be a white. This is a good woman, the one your father has found?"

"I think so." He would not answer her fully. He still felt a little reservation about Miss Green.

"No matter what your mother says, you must remember that you have another home," she told him earnestly. "Blood cannot be washed away by pretending it is not there."

"I wanted to go to the Klamath Reservation and see my mother. But my father keeps me working every day." Even as he spoke he remembered Sundays. Why hadn't he gone to see his mother on one of those occasions when Pa was taking Miss Green for a long buggy ride? The next time it happened, that's what he would do. It would mean a whipping afterwards, but Billy didn't care. Seeing Tobey made him realize just how much he missed his mother.

"She is not there." Tobey shook her head. "Kientepoos—Captain Jack—has taken his people back to their old home on the Lost River."

"But why? I thought everything was going well."

"When the snow left, the Modocs began cutting new railroad ties. This time they had three hundred before the Klamaths came and hauled them away. The young braves wanted war, but Jack persuaded them to wait. He went again to the agent to ask protection. The agent had him thrown out of his office. He closed his ears and told Jack not to bother him again."

Billy stared at her without speaking. That such an indignity had been done to the Chief of the Modocs was beyond words.

"So now your mother is home. The Modocs are all home on the Lost River. I hope they will be permitted to stay," concluded Tobey. "She wanted you to know."

After she had gone, Billy went about his chores with a troubled heart. A traveler brought in his horse to be stabled for the night. He rubbed the animal down and put it in a stall with a supper of oats. He finished the job he had begun earlier, cleaning out the stalls, and checked a harness that Pa had told him showed signs of wear. He didn't think of any of these things while he was doing them. He thought only of his mother's people and how happy they must be to be at home.

When the afternoon shadows lengthened into evening, he locked the doors for the night and returned home. There he built up the fire and began preparing the evening meal. When it was cooked, he ate his share and set Pa's back to keep warm. It didn't occur to him to worry about the hour. Pa could take care of himself. Maybe he'd eaten at the Greens' and on his return had gone straight to his nightly duties as deputy sheriff.

Pa arrived at the cabin well after dark and looking as proud as a youth who has just killed his first bear.

"It's all fixed, Billy boy," he shouted happily. "I done it and she said yes."

"You mean Miss Green?" Billy wondered why he felt suddenly cold, as though the north wind had just blown through the cabin.

"That's right." Pa beamed as he reached below the built-in bed in one corner and pulled out the jug that he always kept hidden there. He took a great swallow that Billy could watch as it went down his throat. "We're going to be married, me and her. And I won't be a squaw man no more, and you won't be a breed. You'll be her son as well as mine. After that, just let them old biddies turn up their noses if they dare."

Chapter Four

PA AND MISS GREEN WERE MARRIED SEVERAL WEEKS later, with practically the whole town in attendance. It was a church wedding and Miss Green wore a white dress and a hat covered with artificial flowers. Pa had a new suit, too, a black one, with pants that matched the jacket. He wasn't too happy about that and grumbled a lot when he had to buy it. There wasn't one in Quincy's general store that fit him so Mr. Quincy had to send away for it, which delayed the wedding. But Miss Green had her heart set on Pa wearing a real suit so they had to wait.

Billy was glad of the delay. In spite of Miss Green's cooking, he couldn't help the stirrings of alarm whenever he thought that soon he would have a new mother. No one suggested that he have a new suit for the occasion, so he wore his old pants and the plaid shirt Pa had bought him. The shirt was beginning to show wear, but he could still get into it.

After the ceremony, there was a reception in the churchyard. A long table, made of boards, had been set up on sawhorses. It was covered with several tablecloths and loaded with food. There were plates of sandwiches filled with roasted meat, pickles, a punch made from strained blackberries, and several cakes. One was covered with white frosting. People said that was the bride's cake, and Miss Green, now Mrs. Morrison, made a great to-do about cutting it herself.

Billy stood awkwardly behind the fringe of guests crowding around the refreshment table and listened to their talk and laughter. No one spoke to him or invited him to step forward and help himself to the food as everyone else was doing. Whenever anyone happened to glance in his direction their eyes passed over him as though he were a bush or a clump of weeds, something that was not worth noticing. Even Pa seemed to have forgotten him, not that Billy blamed him for it. It was Pa's big day. Next to becoming deputy sheriff, marrying Miss Green was probably the most important thing that had ever happened to him.

He felt terrible standing there, and finally he turned and left. No one seemed to notice. At least, no one called after him.

There was one thing he could do for Pa and his new wife on their wedding day. He could clean up the cabin, make it as neat as he could. In their haste that morning, they had left dirty dishes, and the bed was still unmade.

He worked for a couple of hours, and in addition to the bed and dishes he swept the floor and carried in wood and water. When the new Mrs. Morrison arrived, she couldn't help but notice how nice things looked.

But the new Mrs. Morrison didn't seem to think

things were nice when her husband proudly ushered her through the door later that afternoon. She stood in the middle of the floor and her eyes took careful inventory of the single room. There was no smiling approval on her face, and the eyes under the flower-trimmed hat were narrowed in speculation.

"First off, it's going to have a good cleaning," she announced. "I'd no idea, Moses, you lived in such a pigsty."

"It ain't as bad as that, Etta," protested Pa mildly, while Billy felt cold, angry hurt creep over him. What would she have thought if he hadn't worked so hard to clean things up? "We been batching it, me and Billy, but it ain't that bad at all."

"No," she agreed grimly. "It's worse than bad. First off, boy, you get that heap of dirty blankets off the bed and toss them in the yard. Lucky I have my own bedding. You'll find it in the box Fred dropped off early today."

Billy was so surprised he could only stare blankly, and Pa had to speak to him.

"You heard your new ma, Billy. Toss out the bed covers."

"Another thing," she declared quickly, spinning on her new black wedding slippers. "I'm not that boy's ma. Anybody with eyes in his head could see that."

"But—but—" sputtered Pa. "What's he to call you?"

"He'll call me Mrs. Etta," she told him crisply. "And don't forget the Mrs. It's a mark of respect."

"But he's my son." Pa's face wore an expression Billy had never seen before, astonishment and perhaps a little fear.

"Maybe. But he's not mine," she insisted. "Now

mind what I said about those blankets. And bring in my box of bedding while you're about it."

Billy did as he was told. He stripped the bed of its blankets and threw them out the door. They weren't really dirty, he thought resentfully. His mother used to wash the bedding regularly, and while he and Pa hadn't bothered since she left, they weren't as bad as Mrs. Etta pretended. He carried in the wooden box which he found waiting in the yard, and he and Pa stood watching while she whipped out sheets, pillows and patchwork quilts.

In the midst of her bed making she paused suddenly.

"Where's *he* going to sleep?" she demanded. "Is there a shed or something?"

"Billy always sleeps in front of the fire," explained Pa. "Just rolls up in a blanket and corks off."

"Not any more," she said firmly. Her not quite blue, not quite gray eyes narrowed to slits. Why she's really ugly, Billy thought, and mean, too. "I won't have a half-grown boy sleeping in the same room with me and my husband, especially on my wedding night."

"Now, Etta," protested Pa. "Billy's a real hard sleeper. He won't bother you none."

"I can go down to the stable," suggested Billy. Almost any place would be better than here with this suddenly frightening woman. He felt a little sorry for Pa. "There's plenty of hay. It'll make a good bed."

"Well—" Pa looked at his new wife nervously. "Just for tonight, Billy. You wouldn't know but womenfolks is kind of touchy, especially on their wedding nights. And mind you come back for breakfast. Reckon it'll be a treat not to have to cook breakfast for yourself no more. Nor wash the dishes afterwards."

46

Life was very different for Billy after that day, and the strangest part was the change which came over Pa. Only in the evenings, when he patrolled the streets and the two saloons as deputy sheriff, was Pa like his former self. Whenever he was around Mrs. Etta, he was almost quiet. He kept his hair and beard neatly trimmed and changed his shirt twice a week. He seldom made a decision himself, but always asked her opinion first, and when they went to church on Sunday he wore the despised wedding suit.

Billy was no longer required to accompany them to church, nor did he move back into the house, although he came there three times a day for meals. They were good meals, too, but there were no leftovers for Bud. Mrs. Etta didn't say much to him while they ate. She filled his plate and when it was empty asked if he wanted more, but most of her remarks were directed to Pa.

As soon as he had finished, Billy went back to the livery stable. He had made himself a comfortable bed in the hayloft, using the blankets Mrs. Etta had discarded so scornfully, and Bud shared it with him every night.

One evening Pa had come in unexpectedly and found Bud there, but to their surprise he hadn't said a word. He just asked if they were warm enough, then he went back to being deputy sheriff. After that Billy didn't try to hide the fact that Bud was staying with him.

"It's just like you're a hired hand," decided Bud wisely. "You work for them and they give you bed and board. Only difference is there's no wages."

Billy nodded soberly. He had thought the same thing himself. Certainly that's the way Mrs. Etta treated him, like a servant.

Summer quickly dissolved into autumn and autumn into winter. The snows were heavy that year. Six inches fell in a single night. It was hard to plough through the drifts to the cabin, and when Billy finally made it one day for the midday meal, his face red and tingling, his feet and hands almost without feeling, Mrs. Etta took notice of the fact.

"There's no sense in the boy making this trip three times a day," she announced. "I fixed up his supper and he can carry it back with him."

"But Etta, it'll be cold." Pa ventured one of his rare disagreements. "Billy ought to have three hot meals."

"He'll still have a hot breakfast and dinner," she assured him. "And it'll save him going out at night. You know yourself, Moses, that's when the cold really sets in, around late afternoon. You don't need to worry about him starving. I got enough supper in this bucket to feed two boys his age."

Pa shook his head but made no further protest. There was nothing he could do about his second wife. Billy sometimes wondered if he wasn't sorry he had got rid of his first one.

He himself was glad to have supper from a bucket. Even if the food was cold, it was pleasanter to share it with Bud than to trudge home and eat silently while Mrs. Etta talked on and on about people in whom he had no interest. Bud, of course, was delighted, especially as Mrs. Etta had kept her promise and the bucket held plenty for two.

They had long talks each evening as they munched their cold bread and meat and pie, mostly about Bud's future.

"Someday I'm going back to Frisco," he told Billy. "Now there's a town. I think I was born there."

"You think? Don't you know?"

"Stands to reason. Whoever borned me left me in a church in Frisco. When somebody found me, they put me in an orphan asylum. I had to live there till I was big enough to strike out on my own."

"How old were you then?"

"Oh, about nine, I guess." Bud paused to scratch his head thoughtfully. He had lice, and once Billy had suggested the Indian remedy of coating his scalp with pitch, but Bud said he'd rather scratch. "I couldn't take it no longer. You had to line up and march everywhere you went, and you had to go plenty. To prayers, to meals, to school, to bed."

"You went to school?" Billy was impressed.

"I had to. I can read some and write a little and do numbers if they ain't too high. Never took much to book learning, but they made us go. So one day I lit out. Lived on the street. There was lots of others like me doing that, so many that the handouts was pretty slim. That's why I come up the coast. Not so many orphans up here and the pickings are better."

"But you want to go back?"

"When I'm bigger. Then I can handle a man's job. Maybe I'll be a sailor. Lots of ships in the harbor. I could sign on easy, soon as I'm bigger. You ought to come with me."

"I don't know—"

"Or we could stick around Barbary Coast. Bet I could get a job tending bar. If you keep on growing the way you are, you could be a bouncer."

"What's that?"

"If somebody in the bar gets out of hand, the

bouncer throws him out," explained Bud kindly. "I'd be one if I could, but I'm not big enough."

Billy looked at him sympathetically. In the past year, Bud hadn't grown much. He would probably always be small and pinched-looking. But he was a friend, a real friend.

Spring finally arrived and the birds began coming back to Klamath Lake. When the snow melted, the grass, hidden so long under a white cover, was green enough to dazzle your eyes in the sunshine. Without the snow as an excuse, Mrs. Etta grudgingly said that Billy could start returning for supper. She actually smiled when he told her he had got used to carrying it in a bucket and would just as soon continue.

She wasn't the only one who smiled these days. For some reason, Pa had recovered his good humor. He didn't roar and give brusque orders as he used to, but he went around with his chest stuck out and a swagger to his walk. One day he told Billy the reason.

"Come next fall, your—Mrs. Etta's going to have a baby," he confided. "You're going to have a little brother, and I'll be a pa again."

Billy didn't answer. He was rubbing down a horse and while he didn't miss a stroke, his mind was racing.

Pa was going to have a new son. An all-white son. The thought that it might be a girl didn't occur to him. Mrs. Etta wouldn't hear of such a thing. No one needed to tell Billy what the addition would do to him. He was little better than a servant now, and with a new son in the family he would lose even Pa's uncertain allegiance. There was only one thing for him to do. He would go to his mother's people, the Modocs. He would say good-bye to Bud and start that very night.

50

Chapter Five

BILLY FITTED THE REED ARROW TIPPED WITH OBSIDIAN
to the sinew string, held the bow in the way Scar Face
Charley had showed him, and pulled back carefully.
The arrow flew free, striking the red circle he had
painted on a target. It hung there, quivering in the
very center, and he gave a little grunt of satisfaction.

"Good," said a voice behind him, and Billy
jumped. He hadn't known anyone was watching.

Captain Jack had come up silently, his slippers of
woven tule making no sound on the hard earth. His expression was serious. Only the eyes in the round, brown
face smiled approval as he looked from the boy to the
tule mat with its painted circles.

"Can you do that again?" he asked.

"Yes," said Billy simply. Now he could strike the
center of the circle each time he aimed, but it had taken
a lot of practice. In the year and a half since he had

lived with the Modocs his days had been spent in practice, not only with the bow, but in learning to paddle the Indian canoes which were used for transportation on the streams and lakes. It had taken practice, too, for him to learn to follow an animal trail, and time and practice for his feet, which had always before worn leather soled shoes to learn the feel of the rocky terrain and grow calloused enough so they didn't bleed when he stepped on the sharp lava fields surrounding Tule Lake.

Children half his age were able to manage the things he needed to know more easily than he, but he was learning. Now his callouses had grown as tough as anyone's. His eyes had learned to pick out and avoid many of the jagged rock shapes, concealed by straggling vegetation, which could set the unwary tumbling to the ground. Yes, he was learning, but he still hadn't learned enough to suit himself or especially Curly Headed Doctor, the medicine man, who decided when a boy should make his quest, after which the boy was considered a man.

"You shoot at a strange target," said Captain Jack thoughtfully.

"It is a white man's target." Billy hung his head. Perhaps the chief thought ill of him for bringing something of the white man's ways to the Modoc village. He had painted the tule mat himself and hung it from a juniper bush to test his skill.

"Some of the white man's ways are good," said Captain Jack. "We should take from them what we can use."

This time he smiled approval with his mouth as well as his eyes, and as he walked away Billy looked after him with something of reverence. Was there ever so fine a man, so great a chief as this one? He doubted it. He walked over to the juniper to retrieve his arrow and resume his practice.

"A boy who shoots at painted circles!" Bogus Charley was waiting for him when he returned. He was laughing, as always, but somehow Billy didn't find his jokes as amusing as he had when he was younger. Now he could see that the jokes were usually at the expense of someone else. "Perhaps that would make a good name for you."

"My name is Billy. Billy Modoc." He looked at the older man steadily. No longer would he use the name of Morrison. That belonged to Pa.

"That is hardly enough. We are all Modocs." Bogus Charley laughed heartily. "Painted Circle Billy. How does that sound?"

Billy made himself shrug indifferently as he refitted the arrow to his bow. If Bogus knew the name was distasteful, he would use it all the more. Soon everyone would call him that.

Again the arrow flew to its mark in the exact center of the target, and Bogus regarded it with respect.

"Who showed you how to shoot?" he asked.

"Scar Face Charley."

This time it was the older man who shrugged. Then he walked away. Scar Face Charley was the best shot and the finest tracker in Captain Jack's band. No one argued with him.

Billy shot one more arrow, but he had lost interest. He retrieved it and returned to his stepfather's lodge.

His mother, Sally, had remarried soon after returning to her own people. Her husband was called Rabbit Ear Dave, and he had accepted his new stepson gladly. Billy knew that custom demanded that his mother remarry right away. The division of work required both a man and a woman to keep a family running. The man hunted, fished and acted as protector, while the woman gathered roots and berries, prepared the meals and made the clothing. The jobs were not interchangeable, and rich men often took two wives.

Deaf Tom was overjoyed at the marriage and moved right into the new household. He had grown too old to fish or hunt and had lived a hand-to-mouth existence since the death of his wife, dependent on the generosity of his friends. Now he had a comfortable home, two meals every day, and a respected place at the fire. An old man could ask for nothing better.

A sagebrush fire was burning in front of the lodge, and Sally was stirring something in an iron pot hanging over it. The black pot had belonged to Mose Morrison, and how she had smuggled it out in her blanket bundle of belongings Billy didn't know. But there it was, the envy of every woman in the village.

"Antelope," his mother told him, smiling as she caught his hungry eyes on the kettle. "The one your father brought in yesterday."

The antelope was being stewed with ipos, a small tuberous plant not too unlike the white man's potato, and various roots of which only the women knew the names.

Billy nodded and sat on the ground beside his grandfather. The late afternoon was growing chilly and he would have liked to wrap himself in his wool blanket, but Deaf Tom had taken it. The ragged gray folds were wrapped securely around the old man's thin frame, and even then he shivered occasionally.

It was the warmest blanket in the family, although not the only one. Deaf Tom and Rabbit Ear Dave had been given blankets when the Modocs first went to the Klamath Reservation. Each person received one blanket, but they were thin and narrow, nothing to compare with the old one Billy had brought from his father's stable. He had left its mate with Bud, who had no blanket at all, and he wondered if Bud still had it and if he were still in Linkville. By now he might have gone to San Francisco, as he always planned, and sailed off in a ship.

Billy missed Bud a lot. While the Modocs were friendly and had accepted him without question, he had made no special friends his own age. Those boys were far beyond him in skills and they had nothing in common with the newcomer. All of them had made their spiritual quests for power and now were considered young men. Curly Headed Doctor wouldn't let Billy make a quest. First he must learn to be a Modoc, to master those rudiments the little boys were being taught. It was humiliating. Billy sat there, staring at the fire and hating Curly Headed Doctor.

His mother gave the stew a final stir and set it back from the flames. Then she went to fetch a cradleboard that was standing by the lodge. The lodge itself was round, made of willow poles covered with tule mats and dried mud, and gathered together at the top so that the whole looked like an inverted bowl. There was only one opening, higher than the ground, that served as door, window and chimney. But it was comfortable inside, and carpeted with woven tule mats.

His mother took a baby from the cradleboard and unwrapped him from a cocoon of rabbit skins. It was Billy's new little half-brother. Still too young to be named, his mother called him Chipmunk, and indeed he did look like one with his bright little eyes and fast waving arms. Billy liked Chipmunk. Sometimes he thought about his other half-brother whom he'd never seen, Pa's and Mrs. Etta's son, back in Linkville and decided he couldn't be half so smart and cute as Chipmunk.

"You will come to the storytelling tonight?" Deaf Tom's head emerged from the gray blanket and he looked at Billy expectantly. Like most deaf people his voice either came out too loud or so low it was hard to understand him.

Billy jumped. This time it had been too loud.

"Ah," he answered, nodding.

"Good," approved his grandfather. "Tonight Curly Headed Doctor will tell the story of Ben Wright."

Since his grandfather couldn't hear, Billy groaned audibly while he made himself continue smiling. That old story again, he thought. At least three times a week Curly Headed Doctor retold the story of Ben Wright's treachery to the Modocs.

It had happened years ago, before Captain Jack was chief, and it marked the beginning of the tribe's animosity toward the whites. Many of the white residents of the little California town of nearby Yreka were friendly toward the Indians, but there was a faction, headed by Ben Wright, who felt the opposite way. One day Wright came to the Modoc village and invited all the braves to a feast. He said he was their friend, and after extending the invitation he went among the women making gifts of beads and looking glasses.

Old Schonchin, who was then the chief, and some of his followers would not attend. They said Ben

Wright was not to be trusted, and Schonchin warned his people not to eat before the white men. About fifty young braves rode to the appointed place, and there they found an ample feast laid out before them.

But someone remembered Schonchin's warning and called out a caution not to take a bite before their hosts. When the Modocs saw that not a white made a move toward the food they knew it was poisoned and refused to eat at all.

Hearing this, Ben Wright drew his gun and shouted, "If they won't eat food let them eat dust."

It was a signal, and the white men began shooting the unarmed Indians. When they had finished, they scalped their victims and rode back to Yreka where a dance was held in their honor. Of the fifty Modoc braves, forty-one were killed that night, while not a white received a scratch.

Billy had heard the white man's version of the same story and knew it had been brought on by a previous Modoc attack upon an emigrant train. Both sides were wrong, he decided, but it did no good to keep the memory fresh by retelling.

He did not say so to his grandfather, who could not hear him anyway. He merely smiled, and Deaf Tom's head disappeared once more into the folds of the gray blanket.

Soon Rabbit Ear Dave appeared, ready for his second meal of the day. It has been a long time since the first, and Billy's stomach was growling. He shook his grandfather gently, for muffled snores were now coming through the blanket.

"How was the shooting this day?" Rabbit Ear Dave sat on the ground beside Billy. He was a kind man, and since he himself was considered only fair with the bow, he had asked Scar Face Charley to help his new stepson.

"I hit the center every time," Billy told him proudly. "Captain Jack saw me and said it was good."

A pleased smile lightened his stepfather's face. He was not a handsome man, and the unusually long, pointed ears which accounted for his name, made him even more unattractive. Billy smiled back, thinking how lucky he was to have Dave for a father. Suppose his mother had chosen someone like Bogus Charley or Hooker Jim? They would have been willing to take her as a second wife, but she had decided on Rabbit Ear Dave. How wise she was.

"Has Scar Face seen you shoot?" asked Dave.

"Not for several days. Someone said he had gone fishing. I am better than when he last saw me."

"He will be proud," said his stepfather. "As I am proud."

Silently they sat watching Sally struggle to lift the heavy pot from the fire. In Linkville, Billy would have hurried to help her, but here he had learned that a man never interfered in the work of a woman. She would have to manage alone.

Deaf Tom came to with a snort. Billy's shake had done no good, but the smell of the stew had penetrated the blanket and now he was wide awake.

"We eat now," he shouted happily.

But their dinner was postponed, for the sounds of a single pony's hooves beating against the hard trail were suddenly audible. All through the village people stopped what they were doing. The pony was being ridden fast, faster than a brave returning home for dinner, faster than a casual traveler. Every eye turned

58

toward the trail above the village and soon the visitor came in view.

It was a woman, a woman with a brown face and streaming dark hair, astride a sweating pony. They recognized her instantly, and Captain Jack stepped forward.

"Kaitch-ka-na," he called. "Welcome, daughter oɪ my brother."

Billy caught his breath. It was Tobey Riddle, wife of Frank Riddle, the only white who had risen above the stigma of squaw man.

With a flurry of calico skirts, Tobey slipped to the ground. Like her bay mare, she was gasping for breath, and for a moment she could not speak. The Modocs eyed her with growing alarm. Although she no longer lived with her people, she had never ceased to be one of them.

"The soldiers are coming," she told them finally, ignoring the rules of politeness which called for a visitor to lead up to his subject through a courteous exchange of pleasantries. "They are coming to take you back to the reservation of the Klamaths. They will be here tomorrow."

At this all the people began to mutter and cry out. They would not go. This was their land. It had belonged to their fathers before them, and it must be here for their children.

Billy told himself he wouldn't go either. The Klamath Reservation was too close to Linkville, and Linkville meant Pa and Mrs. Etta.

"It has been two years since we left the land of the Klamaths," argued Captain Jack. "The soldiers have left us alone all that time. We live in peace with the white men who have settled on Modoc land. No one has cared that we are here. Why should they care now?"

"A talking paper came from the Great White Father in Washington." By now Tobey was beginning to regain her breath. "The paper says you must return. This time you go to the village at Yainax. It is at the far end of the Klamath land. Thirty of our people live there now, under old Chief Schonchin. They dwell peacefully, and many miles divide them from the Klamath tribe."

"My brother, the once chief, is so old he thinks like a woman." This was Schonchin John, second in command to Captain Jack. Billy had wondered sometimes if Schonchin John did not resent being passed over for a younger man when his elder brother was decreed too old to lead. But he gave no sign of it. He was older than many of the braves, but still vigorous and without fear.

"We have asked the Great White Father to give us land of our own on Lost River," said Jack stubbornly. "He has yet to make reply."

"This is your reply," said Tobey sadly. "The soldiers come to take you to Yainax. They will take you peacefully, if you will, or by force. I beg that you will choose peace. There are as many white soldiers as there are stars in the sky. If you shoot one down, another will take his place."

"My people will decide," Jack told her calmly. "There is another Modoc village across the hill at Nuh-sult-gar-ka. Your brother, Charley, is there. Will you warn them yourself, Kaitach-ka-na, or shall I send a messenger while you take food?"

"There is no time for food," she answered. "I have ridden fifty-eight of the white man's miles today. My

mare will go a little farther. I will carry the warning."
She paused as she prepared to mount and looked over
her shoulder. "The white men do not know that I have
sounded the alarm. But you are my people and close to
my heart. I hope that I see you again."

Billy felt a strange stirring within him at her
words. He knew, even before he heard the shouted cries
of "Fight," "Fight the white soldiers," what the decision would be. It wasn't that he disagreed, but he hoped
he could do his share in battle like a man. Silently he
gave thanks to Scar Face Charley for helping him with
his marksmanship. He would have to use a bow. He
had no gun, and there were no extras. Besides, he had
never shot a gun.

When the tumult died down, Captain Jack called
a council of the elders. After much deliberation, their
decision was to fight and even Captain Jack reluctantly
agreed. It was one thing to make war, another to defend yourself. Besides, he added hopefully, when the
soldiers saw the Modocs were armed and firm in their
resolve, they might give up.

After that he sent a group of braves, headed by
Bogus Charley and including Hooker Jim, Curly
Headed Doctor and Captain Jack's half-brother Black
Jim, to warn the white settlers who had taken up homesteads across the river on the east bank to stay inside
their houses tomorrow. They were to be told that soldiers were coming and there would be a battle. If they
stayed indoors without taking part, no Modoc would
harm them. After the warning, everyone was to return
to the village except Hooker Jim and a handful of
pickèd warriors. They were to remain on the east bank.
It was wise, insisted Captain Jack, to divide forces,
and his sub-chief, Schonchin John, agreed.

Meanwhile, four mounted scouts were sent to bar the road leading from Fort Klamath, there to warn the soldiers to turn back. If their efforts failed, they were to return swiftly and sound the alarm.

"The rest of you, go on with your meal," concluded Captain Jack. "It may be the last hot food you have for a few days. The soldiers cannot arrive before morning."

As they returned to their lodge, Sally said softly to Billy, "The chief could have sent you with the party to warn the settlers. You speak the white man's tongue better than anyone in the village."

Billy didn't answer. The same idea had occured to him, but he didn't like to say so.

"It is because he is still a boy," Rabbit Ear Dave told her, and at the words Billy felt a rush of new resentment against Curly Headed Doctor.

Someday, he told himself, I'll show him! I'll show Curly Headed Doctor that it takes more than a successful quest for power to make a man.

Chapter Six

THE MODOCS WERE LATE GETTING TO BED. ALL EVENING armed braves from Nuh-sult-gar-ka village had been riding in. Warned by Tobey Riddle, they had arrived to add their strength to the band of defending warriors. A few from the village, they reported scornfully, had packed their belongings and were already on their way to Yainax where they would be safe. But these, according to the braves, were old and useless anyway, and the guns and ammunition they owned had been taken from them before they set out.

When it appeared the last of them had arrived, the Modocs climbed into their lodges, prepared to settle down for the night.

"How can they sleep?" Billy asked his stepfather in surprise. "What if the soldiers should come?"

"Battles are not fought in the hours of darkness. They start at dawn and we shall be awake by then,"

Rabbit Ear Dave told him tolerantly. "You will learn all that after you have made your quest. Besides, the soldiers may not come. The scouts may send the soldiers away."

"Now is the time for sleep," said Sally severely. "Let us hear no more of your boy talk."

Billy obediently closed his eyes and was silent, but his mind was racing. Perhaps it was his white blood that told him soldiers did not wait for dawn to make an attack. And as for the scouts, there were only four of them. What chance had they against an army?

He had barely got to sleep when he was awakened by a great tumult outside the lodge. Every dog was barking, and the Modocs had many dogs. Horses were neighing. Men were shouting. Billy threw back his blanket and was up in an instant.

There was a scramble to reach the door opening, but he was the first one there, his bow and a mink-skin quiver of arrows over his shoulder. Briefly, he congratulated himself on not unstringing his bow last night, although Scar Face Charley had assured him it must be done without fail lest the sinew lose its tautness.

After the blackness of the lodge, the stars gave enough light for him to see. The scouts had returned, their horses rearing and pulling on their nettle-fiber guide ropes, but right behind them were the soldiers. Billy thought he could even make out the glint of polished buttons on their coats.

Sleepy-eyed Modocs, most of them carrying rifles and revolvers, were jumping from door openings. In the starlight, the dozen or so lodges looked like a cluster of conical beehives as they disgorged their occupants.

"What is this?" demanded Captain Jack angrily. He confronted one of the soldiers who had stepped forward from the armed ranks. Bogus Charley joined the chief as interpreter.

Billy, who could understand both languages, listened carefully to what the white soldier would reply. Part of him hoped that Bogus would make a mistake, but he didn't.

"My men and I have come to take your people back to the Klamath Reservation," said the soldier, and Billy decided that he must be the officer in charge. "You may go peacefully or by force. We are here to make sure you go."

"My people do not want to go to the land of the Klamaths," Jack replied haughtily. "Once we respected the wishes of the white man and went there because they asked us to. We made peace with our old enemies, and we still keep the peace. But the only way we could keep it was by leaving that place which does not belong to us and returning to land which is ours. Our fathers and their fathers before them held this land. Then there were many of my people, more than there are today. The Modocs have grown smaller in number, and we do not need so much land. We are willing to share some with the whites who come, but here you must let us live out our years."

"I can't do that." Billy thought he caught a note of sympathy in the officer's voice. "I have my orders to take you back."

"Are we dogs that you would drive us before you in that way?" demanded Captain Jack bitterly. "We are not dogs. We are Modocs."

"At least you are live Modocs," answered the officer. "You'll be dead ones if you don't put down your guns. Look around you, chief. Every one of your men is covered by a rifle."

Captain Jack turned and his eyes moved around the encircling soldiers. Billy did the same. The muzzle of a rifle was aimed at each individual Modoc. Why, there was even one pointed at him!

Captain Jack and Schonchin John exchanged glances.

"I will go," agreed the chief reluctantly. "I will take my people with me, but I no longer believe what the white man tells me."

"Just put your guns down there on the ground," ordered the officer, ignoring Captain Jack's opinion of the white man's lack of truth. "I don't want to hurt anybody."

Jack hesitated. "Why should I do that?"

"You are the chief. If you lay down your arms, all your men will do the same."

"This man wants to do to us what Ben Wright did to the Modocs years ago," called one of the older Modocs.

"Why do you want to disarm my people?" asked Jack. "I have never yet fought the white man. I have always spoken for peace. Some of my men are afraid of what you ask me to do."

"It is good that you do not want to fight the soldiers," said the officer when Bogus had translated. "If you believe what you say, you will give up your guns. No one will be harmed."

After a moment of hesitation, the chieᶠ threw his rifle on the ground, then his revolver. Silently, one by one, the other warriors did the same.

But I won't give up my bow, thought Billy, clutching it against his body. Luckily no one asked him to.

The sky behind the camp was fading to the color of the inside of a shell, and the dark masses that had been Modoc lodges and clumps of sagebrush began taking definite detail. Dawn was on its way.

Suddenly one of the white scouts gave a shout.

"There's a party of Modocs camped across the river. I'll go route the varmints out."

Bogus Charley had not caught what he said, but Billy heard. The white officer heard, too, and with an annoyed exclamation ordered some of his troops to accompany the departing man.

At the same moment there came a terrifying war whoop from the riverbank. Even the disarmed braves jumped, while the soldiers raised their rifles.

Scar Face Charley and the three men who had accompanied him on a fishing expedition had returned. Now they came loping up the bank, flourishing their rifles. They stopped short, staring at the sullen-faced Modocs, the line of armed soldiers.

"Are these your men?" the officer asked Captain Jack curtly. "Then tell them to put their guns on the pile with the others."

Bogus relayed the message, and after a minute three of the men obeyed. Scar Face Charley was reluctant to give up his rifle.

"This good gun. Belong me." He spoke a little broken English and addressed the officer himself. His hands caressed the barrel of the rifle before he gently put it on the pile.

"Now your revolver. The one you've got strapped on your leg," ordered the white man.

Scar Face shook his head stubbornly.

"You got gun. Pistol belong me. Me no shoot him you."

One of the young officers stepped forward. His face was reddened with anger at what he considered the Modoc's insolence.

"Here, Injun. Give me that pistol, and do it quickly."

Scar Face laughed.

"Me no dog. You talk like me dog. Me man. You talk me good. Maybe me listen."

Billy caught his breath as he saw the young officer's hand move to the holster at his side. Scar Face saw it, too, and his own revolver was out at the same instant. Both men fired together, making a single report. A second later Scar Face leaped toward the stack of rifles and had his own off the top. There was a mad scramble as other Modocs followed his example.

The soldiers were too stunned by the sudden events to take immediate aim. By the time they had rallied, the Indians had scattered into the thick sagebrush behind the camp where their women, children and old people had long since taken refuge. From there they could shoot at the soldiers in the open, while the whites had only puffs of smoke and an occasional lifted head at which to take aim.

Shooting had begun across the river shortly after the first exchange of pistol shots. Billy didn't think about that, or the battle going on in front of him. He was only concerned with what had happened to Scar Face. He was still alive or he couldn't have raced for his rifle, but was he badly wounded? Billy hoped not. Scar Face had been good to him while he was perfecting his bowmanship.

"You waste your arrows. They will not shoot that far." The voice came from the sage brush to his right. The next minute he heard the sounds of a rifle being reloaded. Then he saw Scar Face Charley's head and shoulders as he took careful aim and fired.

"You are not hurt?" Billy cried joyfully.

"Nearly got scalped." His voice was cheerful, even in the face of such near disaster. "The white man's bullet put a hole in the handkerchief I had over my head. It took a little hair, but that is nothing. I will grow more hair, but I may never get another red handkerchief."

Billy began to laugh nervously. He thought his voice had finished changing, but at the moment it reverted and he heard himself laughing in the high tenor of a girl.

"You are becoming good with the bow," said Scar Face. His tone was conversational, as though he and Billy were speaking alone and not in the midst of battle. "But an arrow will not shoot this far."

"I can hit a target almost every time." Billy forced himself to stop laughing.

"What you need next is a gun." Scarface raised to shoot again. As soon as he resumed his place, he continued talking. "I will get you one when this is over. There will be dead soldiers with guns lying about."

"Look!" cried Billy. "A fire!"

Scar Face raised himself to stare where the boy was pointing, then settled back to swear softly to himself. It went on a long time, and Billy finally interrupted impatiently.

"What is it?"

"The whites are burning our village," Scar Face told him bitterly. "I hope everyone was out."

"I think so. The women and children left before you came. What will we do now?"

"Wait. Captain Jack will send scouts. When it is

safe to come out, he will let us know."

It seemed hours until the signal came for the scattered Modocs to emerge from their hiding places. When they did, they found their lodges reduced to smoldering ashes and the soldiers gone. They had taken the Indians' canoes and carried their own dead and wounded with them. As near as the Modocs could figure, at least seven soldiers had been killed outright, and there were more wounded than they could account for.

On the Modoc side, one fifteen-year-old girl had been killed, as well as one old woman and two small children. A single warrior, Wish-in-push, was slain, and Skukum Horse was wounded but not fatally. Curly Headed Doctor said he would make medicine and have him well in no time.

A scout reported that Hooker Jim's men had been attacked by the very settlers who had promised to stay away from the battle, and now Hooker Jim and his followers were advancing on the homesteads, swearing death to every man.

Captain Jack shook his head sadly when he heard. "I hope he will remember that Modocs do not kill women and children," he said.

"He will remember," the scout assured him. "He told me to tell you that, and that he will meet you in the appointed place."

"What place?" asked Bogus Charley quickly. "Have you prepared for this?"

"We have prepared," said Schonchin John.

"We will go to the Modoc Stronghold in the lava beds," added Captain Jack. "No one can move us from there."

Chapter Seven

IT WAS NOT THE FIRST TIME BILLY HAD BEEN TO THE Modoc Stronghold in the lava beds, and although he had never thought of it as a fortress, he could see now that it was ideal for that purpose.

It was a mountainous mass of fractured lava rock, circular in shape, with but a single opening which was approached by a rough, jagged trail winding upward to the top. Each side of the trail was protected by craggy outcroppings of rock which left peep holes for the eye or the muzzle of a rifle. Man himself could never have built a better fortress, for the top was encircled by a deep trench left by the cooling lava. The inner sides were studded with caves, tubular in shape and varying in size, in which the people could make temporary homes. At the very bottom of the inner circle was a level space large enough for the Modocs to hold councils or war dances.

The fortress was set in the midst of what looked, from a distance, to be miles of undulating plain, but was really crushed lava in which sturdy rock plants and bunch grass had somehow taken root. It was treacherous underfoot, as Billy had discovered on his first visit. Only someone well trained in crossing such terrain could manage it without skinned knees and feet shredded by sharp rock. In the winter months mule deer came from the mountains to graze on the vegetation, and it was the year around home of small animals like rabbits.

The blue waters of Tule Lake, called Mo-wa-too by the Modocs, lapped only a few yards from the entrance, with a peninsula of rock running down from the Stronghold close to the water some distance away. A series of bluffs stretched three to five miles to one side, offering the only protection for the soldiers should they follow to set up camp.

As soon as they reached the Stronghold, Captain Jack began making preparations for the siege he knew would follow. He sent hunters to the lake to bring in any waterfowl that had paused to rest on their winter migration. Others carried nets and fishing spears. The majority of the men and boys were set to building breastworks above the trench, piling up boulders so the warriors would have protection during an attack.

Billy was chosen for this. He went at it wholeheartedly although he would rather have been one of the hunters. What he resented was Curly Headed Doctor's self-appointed task. He was weaving a long rope of tule reeds as fast as the women could gather them from the water's edge and bring them to him. He said it would be a magic rope and must be long enough to encircle the whole fortress. When it was finished, he would say special words that would protect the occupants from harm.

Billy never doubted the powers of the magic rope, but he thought some of the tules could be used to make needed things like sleeping mats and cooking baskets. The Modocs had lost everything they owned when the soldiers burned their village. Only Billy's blanket was safe. Deaf Tom had wrapped it around himself as he came from the lodge. Now he claimed it as his own property.

On the day after their arrival at the Stronghold, Hooker Jim and his party caught up with them. They boasted that they had killed seventeen white settlers. They had obeyed their chieftain's orders and the dead were all male, but they had made the women and children watch while their husbands and fathers were slaughtered. They brought two beef carcasses, taken from the settlers' herds, which the women immediately took over. Some of it was cooked for the next meal, but the largest part was cut into strips and hung on improvised racks above a drying fire in one of the caves. If their chief was right about the soldiers coming, the tribe might need dried meat before the siege was ended.

A few days later they were joined by a group of Hot Creek Modocs who lived some distance away. Their village was adjacent to land occupied by a white man named John Fairchild, who regularly paid them a small sum for the privilege of settling there. The story they had to tell made Billy shiver, for it brought back memories of the cold-eyed citizens of Linkville.

Fairchild had convinced the Hot Creeks that they could only be safe if they went to Yainax while the trouble with Jack's people was going on. Led by Fairchild himself, they had almost reached the ferry crossing on the Klamath River when they met Mr. Dyer, the new Indian agent, and an irate party of men from Linkville who demanded the Hot Creeks be turned over to them.

Fairchild refused and drew his revolver. In the heated dispute between the whites, the Hot Creeks simply melted away in the surrounding pine forest. The angry faces of the whites had not been hard to read. By a circuitous route they made their way to the lava beds and their own people.

Captain Jack was pleased. Fourteen of the Hot Creeks were fighting men and he now had fifty-six warriors in the Stronghold.

Billy was pleased, too. One of the Hot Creek Modocs was close to his age. Although he was clearly one of the fighting men, a warrior, he seemed friendly. He had picked Billy out and kept smiling at him all the while the others were talking. From his place behind the warriors, Billy smiled back. It felt good to be singled out.

When the council was over and preparations were underway for the welcoming dance, the young warrior walked over to him.

"I am called Ellen's Man," he announced. He had a round face with as yet no signs of unsightly hair that must be plucked out, and he never seemed to stop smiling.

"I am Billy. Billy Modoc."

"Is that all?" Ellen's Man seemed surprised.

"Isn't it enough?" Billy wondered if he had made a mistake. Perhaps Ellen's Man might prove to be the kind who was always finding fault.

"Oh, yes," agreed Ellen's Man hastily. "I am called

Ellen's Man because I was left an orphan and Ellen adopted me. When I was of an age, she married me, so now I am truly Ellen's Man. Shacknasty Jim is called so because his mother keeps her lodge so dirty. Steamboat Frank married a woman of tremendous size who puffs and blows like one of the white man's noisy canoes. Perhaps someday you will get a new name of your own."

"Perhaps." Billy began to smile again. There was nothing critical or fault-finding about Ellen's Man. He might even be a little simple.

"You are a warrior?" he asked hesitantly. When Ellen's Man found that he, himself, was not, it could be the end of a budding friendship.

"Of course. I am a great fighter. I never give up. Only if the enemy kills me will I give up. I have been in two battles. How many battles have you been in?"

"Only the one when the soldiers attacked our camp. And that didn't count. I am not a warrior. I have not had my quest for power." Billy decided he might as well make a full confession. Ellen's Man would find out sometime, and it might as well be now.

"Why not?" Ellen's Man looked puzzled. "You are big enough. You are taller than I and your shoulders are even wider. Did you make a quest and were refused the power?"

"No." Billy denied it quickly. "Curly Headed Doctor says I am not ready. I am half white and I lived with whites until just over a year ago. When I came to my mother's village I didn't know anything, how to shoot an arrow, how to walk properly, how to track. I knew none of the stories of our people or their songs and dances. Curly Headed Doctor said I must learn all these things before I make a quest."

"Do you know them now?" The smooth brown face wrinkled thoughtfully. Ideas took root slowly in his brain.

"Yes."

"Then you must make a quest!" Ellen's Man told him triumphantly. Again his face was wreathed in happy smiles. "I made my quest early. Earlier than other boys. I grew fast. Ellen said I was ready. She is always right. The power came to me on the second day. It is very strong."

"I don't think Curly Headed Doctor would let me make a quest," Billy told him unhappily. "Not when the soldiers are coming."

"Then you will have to fight without power," decided Ellen's Man. "But do not worry. It will not take long to whip the white man. Then you can make your quest. But be careful. It is dangerous to go into battle without power. I would not want you to be killed."

Several weeks went by and still no soldiers came to storm the Stronghold. Scouts reported that two camps had been set up on the bluffs, one a soldier camp five or six miles almost due east of the Stronghold, the other a camp of volunteers about fifteen miles due west. The scouts also saw loaded wagons making the trip on the winding, torturous road between. Since loaded wagons meant supplies, food, clothing and more importantly, ammunition, Jack sent out raiding parties.

Billy was not selected to take part in any of the raids, but Ellen's Man went. Once the raiders returned with heavy boxes loaded with ammunition that could not be used in their ancient guns. Another time they brought back several canteens, more ammunition and a case of whiskey. They recovered no food, and the Modocs had to depend on mule deer which the hunters provided and the few birds that had not left the lake.

Two sentries stood guard day and night on the ledge atop the Stronghold, and Billy was expected to take his turn at that. It was an uncomfortable duty, for now they were coming into winter. The wind was bitingly cold, so cold he sometimes thought it would freeze the blood in his veins. There were frequent snowstorms, and what was worse, sometimes hail and sleet that stung like insect bites when they hit his un-protected face.

He was standing guard one morning when he thought he saw movement on the top of the bluffs. The day had dawned surprisingly clear and in the crisp, pure air the distance between the Stronghold and the bluffs seemed much closer than it really was. He nar-rowed his eyes and stared again before calling the sec-ond guard.

"A supply wagon?" asked Pete Schonchin, son of the Modoc sub-chief, who was sharing the duty.

"I do not think so." Billy shook his head, straining his eyes at the tiny dots. "I think it is horsemen, a long party."

Pete squinted carefully.

"It is horsemen," he agreed. "You have Modoc eyes."

"I am a Modoc," Billy reminded him stiffly. Pete was one of the boys who had made a successful quest for power the summer before. There was a great gulf between them.

"I know you are." Pete sounded a little embar-rassed. "You report this to Captain Jack. You saw them before I did."

When he heard Billy's report the chief sent out scouts to see what the white soldiers were doing. The

Modocs knew the lava beds intimately, the location of each sizeable boulder and every tall thicket of sagebrush. They could creep freely from one protection to the next and keep their presence hidden.

When the scouts returned they reported that the soldiers were no longer sitting idly in camp. There were two great armies preparing for war, one of volunteers, one of walking soldiers. Horses were not to be employed in this battle. But it was unlikely that anything would happen until the following day for the men were busy cleaning guns, sharpening their long knives and making other preparations.

Captain Jack also made his preparations. The women were sent after great armloads of dry sagebrush for the fires and to bring in supplies of water from the lake. The hunters brought in another mule deer. When the council fire was blazing, every warrior was summoned.

Since Billy was not recognized as a warrior, he could not sit in the first circles, but he found a place behind the privileged braves where he could see and hear everything that was said. The first to speak was Captain Jack.

"My people," he began. "I do not want this war. The Modocs are brave and strong. Here in our Stronghold we are protected from the bullets of the white man. We may kill all the soldiers who come tomorrow. It will not matter, for even more will come to take their places. But when a Modoc dies, there is none to take his place. We cannot stay here in the rocks forever. There is still time to make peace with the white man."

He had barely finished when Schonchin John

jumped to his feet. His big head was thrust forward from his burly shoulders, and Billy realized that the sub-chief's Indian name Skoncnes, which was the same as Schonchin, meaning "sticks out head," was aptly given. His brown face was seamed with many lines and his heavy brows lowered over his eyes in the same way as Pa's when he was feeling mean.

"I am a Modoc," he cried angrily. "We are all Modocs here. The white man is our enemy. He has come to our land to take it from us. Maybe we will die, but we will take many white men with us. I say there can be no peace."

Scar Face Charley spoke next.

"My brothers." He raised his voice to still a murmur of agreement caused by Schonchin John's words. "When we fought on the Lost River my blood was hot from the words of the white soldier. Now it has cooled and I see things more clearly. There is wisdom in what your chief has said. We cannot whip all the whites. Some of them have been our friends, and I do not want to fight them. But I am not afraid to die. If our people say war, then I will fight."

Curly Headed Doctor spoke last, and Billy listened to him resentfully. The medicine man would have no place in the battle. Why should he be allowed to speak?

"Some of the words spoken have been women's words," he declared scornfully. "Are the Modocs women? My magic rope has kept the Stronghold safe. This night I will make even greater magic. I will make a medicine flag to fly above the Stronghold. It is the greatest protection of all. If you are Modocs your hearts are brave. You will fight the enemy tomorrow."

Captain Jack then called for a vote of the assembled warriors, and only fourteen made the sign for peace. The remainder signed for war against the whites.

"The people have spoken," announced Jack. "Tomorrow when the soldiers come we will fight to the end."

Chapter Eight

WITH THE COMING OF DAWN, THE MODOCS DISCOVERED that Curly Headed Doctor's medicine was very strong indeed. During the night a dense fog had rolled in off the lake, concealing the lava beds in thick, white dampness. Although it hid the bluffs where the soldiers had made their camp, the Modocs knew that the upper slopes would be bathed in watery sunshine and in all likelihood the army would set out as planned. The warriors took their positions on the ledge to wait.

It took some time for the soldiers to arrive, and the fog showed no signs of lifting. Even Modoc eyes could not penetrate the white blanket, but it did not matter. Their ears told them all they needed to know.

A bugle, muffled by the low-lying dampness, sounded, as though coming from the lake itself, and the next moment there was a low rumble to the east. The divided enemy was advancing on them from two directions at once.

But it was an enemy without eyes, Billy told himself, and without ears as well. It had taken long months of concentrated effort for him to bring his own hearing near the standard of the tribesmen, and even now, he admitted reluctantly, it fell short. White men did not know how to make the most of the senses the god Ka-moo-kum-chux had given them.

He was standing at one of the smaller peepholes in the ledge, an unimportant one that gave him limited view, and he was lucky to have that. He had no gun and all the strategic openings in the breastwork were occupied by warriors with rifles.

Then his ears brought him a word he knew.

"Charge!" It was an English word and came out of the billowing whiteness and was followed by another bugle call.

Fog-shrouded shapes began staggering from the center of the mist, teetering shapes, for the lava-covered ground was rough and it was hard for heavy-soled boots to maintain a balance. At once Modoc rifles cracked from the rocky fortress, and the shapes began to tumble, one by one. Still they kept coming, those ghostlike shapes that almost seemed to float out of the white curtain, hesitate a moment, then crumple to the ground.

The Modocs had only old muzzle-loading rifles which had to be reloaded after each shot, but there was plenty of time. Billy remembered the stories he had heard in Linkville, sneering remarks about how poorly the Indian handled a gun. It was not true. The Modocs, at least, were good marksmen.

There was another bugle call and the advance was halted. Now the army fired from within the concealing fog. They could not see to take aim, but fired blindly at the Stronghold, trying to follow the sounds of Modoc gunfire. Spasmodic bursts of light flickered in the cloud, but the bullets crashed harmlessly against the rock.

The shooting went on all morning. By midday the fog still hung thick and concealing, and Captain Jack gave the order for his own men to stop returning the fire. They must waste no more ammunition. They would have to get closer to the enemy.

He called to some of his own Lost River Modocs, men who were known for their skill as sharpshooters, to follow him to the rocky point running down toward the lake. Almost before he finished speaking, Ellen's Man began naming Hot Creek Modocs to join the party. Billy stared at him in surprise. How could one so young presume to speak for the older warriors? He could tell by the faces of his own tribesmen that they were as surprised as he. The Hot Creeks did not seem to question Ellen's Man, however. They stepped forward, clutching their rifles, as their names were called.

"To that one must have been given special power," said Curly Headed Doctor. He spoke softly, but his words were overheard by one of the older Hot Creeks who remained behind to defend the Stronghold.

"That is so," he answered proudly. "As long as Ellen's Man lives, no Hot Creek will fall in battle."

As the enemy, quick to notice that the Modocs had ceased firing, cheered and again began cautiously coming forward so they were visible, the fortress defenders resumed their task of picking them off, one by one.

Billy now had a peephole which gave an unobstructed view. Not that there was anything to see, he told himself resentfully. Nothing but cloudy whiteness, with an occasional gray shape that either fell to the ground or darted back into concealment. He wished that he could have been one of the party now creeping down the incline, circling the Stronghold and stealing through the fog to the rocky peninsula that separated the army of soldiers from the army of volunteers.

They knew when the warriors had arrived at their destination, for a tremendous war whoop reached the Stronghold. After that, firing from the rocky point predominated. The enemy must have decided it was useless to attack the Stronghold any longer. It was maddening to hear the battle going on so close and yet be ignorant of what was happening. Billy wished that the warriors had taken the new medicine flag with them, but it still hung limply on the highest point above the fortress. The flag was made of mink skin, hawk feathers and a special medicine bead, but its protective power lay in the special chants and dances Curly Headed Doctor had performed while he was making it. He claimed it was the strongest medicine anyone could make, and perhaps its power was great enough to follow the warriors to the point. At least, Billy told himself practically, the Modocs had one advantage. They had the rocks to hide behind, while the whites fought in the open.

The afternoon wore on. Then the bugle sounded once again and the firing stopped. Billy knew, without being told, that the enemy was retreating. They were going back to their camps. Still he stayed at his peephole, as did the others, straining his eyes in a futile effort to see.

An hour later, the fog lifted briefly. The sun was just disappearing behind the mountains to the west. Its last rays fell on a field littered with dead and wounded men. Billy could see that the Modocs were now coming from their hiding places in the rocks. They waved their rifles triumphantly to the watchers in the fortress, a signal that there had been no casualties among them.

He looked toward the west. Stumbling along the trail that led to the tents on the bluffs, he could see a straggling line of soldiers. Some of them carried litters for their wounded comrades, and they walked slowly, painfully, as though their feet were sore. The edges of sharp lava had cut through the leather of their shoes. There was no sign of the volunteers. They must have retreated earlier.

The Modoc women began building up a great fire in the center of the Stronghold. There would be much to celebrate that night, and the one to boast loudest would be Curly Headed Doctor. He had started already.

"I told you my medicine was strong," he shouted. "Never doubt it. The Modocs are fortunate that they have me as their medicine man."

Just as the triumphant warriors returned to the Stronghold, the fog closed in again, but it did nothing to dampen the victory dance.

In the morning it had lifted completely. The Modoc warriors and some of the women went into the battlefield seeking the spoils of war. Billy did not go with them. Since he had no part in the battle, he did not feel he had the right.

They returned in a few hours, each loaded down with loot. They had taken clothing from the bodies of the dead, canteens, and the contents of pockets. But most important, they had guns and cartridge belts.

The soldiers had taken the rifles of the dead and wounded with them, but many of the volunteers, unused to battles of this nature, had dropped everything that might impede their progress as they made a hasty retreat. The Modocs now had Spencer sporting rifles, Remington and Ballard rifles, as well as a few old-patent Henry rifles. Now there was use for the ammunition captured from the wagon train. In addition, the ground had been scattered with more ammunition, which was carefully gathered up. There were also army hats discarded here and there, so many hats that everyone in the tribe could have one.

Billy put his on because it was handed to him, but he took no pride in it. The sight of all those dead men lying on the field had left him with a funny feeling in his stomach.

Later, soldiers came under a white flag and carried away their fallen comrades. It would have been easy to pick them off, and some of the Modocs suggested doing so, but Captain Jack would not permit it.

"Let them have their dead," he ordered sternly. "Are we dogs to snarl over carcasses?"

Billy was glad to hear him speak in such a way. Now that he looked back on yesterday it had been a horrifying experience. He had not fully realized that those dark shapes emerging from the fog were men, brave men at that. But he forgot about it when Scar Face Charley sought him out.

Billy was sitting on the floor of his stepfather's cave, waiting for his mother to finish preparing their morning meal, when Charley's tall figure darkened the opening.

"I have kept my promise," he announced, smiling. The morning sun picked out the jagged scar that puckered his thin cheek from one eye to below his nose.

Billy scrambled to his feet and automatically

caught the rifle that Scar Face tossed to him. His fingers ran up and down the cool metal of the long muzzle and he stared at it in disbelief.

"But I am not a warrior," he protested. "I have not made my quest."

"You will." Scar Face Charley nodded. Then he turned and walked away.

Chapter Nine

THE MOON HAD BEEN A THIN CRESCENT ABOVE THE LAVA beds when the white armies attacked the Stronghold. Every night it rose in the east a little larger until it was as round as the sacred circle, then it began to diminish and finally was gone altogether. It reappeared as a crescent once more before the Modocs had another contact with their enemy.

On that day the sentinels reported three riders approaching on the trail beside the lake. They carried the white flag, which meant that they were unarmed, and Captain Jack sternly ordered his warriors to hold their fire. As the riders came close enough to recognize, he leaned his own rifle against the rocks and started down the path to meet them.

"Who is it?" Billy asked his stepfather curiously.

Although Rabbit Ear Dave was not always an accurate marksman, no one had keener eyesight.

"It is Kaitch-ka-na," he answered, frowning. "With her are the two whites from Yreka for whom our chief has the most respect. Their names are Steele and Roseborough. I have seen them often in the white man's village."

Apparently Captain Jack's regard for the whites was not shared by everyone, for, as Rabbit Ear Dave said their names, grunts of disapproval came from several Modocs.

Before long their chief reappeared, followed by Tobey Riddle and the two white men. Glimpses of white shirts and neckties were visible at the throats of their bulky overcoats, and their trousers were stuffed into the tops of sturdy boots. Woolen caps were pulled down over their ears and Billy looked at the caps jealously. Once he had owned a cap like that. He wished he had it now. The wind still blew fiercely from the snow mountain.

"These are my guests." Jack's dark eyes moved around the circle of sullen faces, and there was no mistaking his meaning. "We will go to the council place to make talk."

Some of the women hurried ahead to throw more sagebrush on the small fire now burning, and the warriors followed close on the heels of the white men.

As Tobey Riddle passed Billy, she hesitated.

"Hello, Billy." She spoke in English.

"Hello." He wished she hadn't singled him out. It made him feel uncomfortable.

"You look well," she said.

"I am well." He answered in the tongue that all Modocs could understand. "Here with my own people I am well and happy."

"Your father misses you." She must have sensed

his wish to be understood by all, for now she too left off speaking English.

"Rabbit Ear Dave is my father now," he told her coldly. "I have no other father."

Tobey smiled faintly and walked on.

Captain Jack sat beside the fire with the two whites at his side. Tobey Riddle stood beside them to interpret, but Bogus Charley was there also to make sure that she spoke true. Schonchin John, Curly Headed Doctor and some of the more prominent Modocs completed the small inner circle, and close behind them was a second circle composed of all the warriors. Billy, resentfully, took his place with the women and children in the rear.

"You are brave to come here," said Scar Face Charley to Tobey. "The white man is our enemy. You have chosen to live with him."

"I am still a Modoc," she answered him serenely. "And Judge Roseborough and Judge Steele have proved their friendship to our people many times."

"Why have you come here?" Jack demanded. His black eyes stared hard at the two men muffled in their heavy coats and woolen caps. "Your people and mine are at war."

"Captain Jack, I am here as your friend," Judge Roseborough told him when Tobey had interpreted the chief's question. "We have been friends for many years. I am your friend in war as well as in peace. Judge Steele is your friend. We did not bring guns with us or any arms. Because we are your friends, we do not need them. We put our faith in you."

"You will not be harmed," Jack promised, and he turned to look meaningly at the second circle. "Life is sweet. I do not take life when it is not necessary. But I

will kill in self-defense. I know my people are doomed.
We are few and the whites are many, but we will defend our own as long as we can."

"Other tribes have given up their lands," Judge
Steele told him. "They were not doomed. The agreement was brought about by peace talks, not war. That
is what we have come to ask you to do. To hold talks
with the whites."

"The whites speak only lies," growled Schonchin
John. "We have heard their lies before."

"Not all whites," corrected Judge Roseborough.
"I have never lied to you."

Billy looked at him carefully. No, he decided, this
man was not like the gimlet-eyed whites he had known
in Linkville. Judge Roseborough's eyes, beneath their
bristly brows, were kind. His mouth was wide and gen-
erous. His thick hair was threaded with gray and extended into mutton chop whiskers down each cheek.
He looked at the other man. Judge Steele was younger.
His eyes were wide set, but they did not turn away as
though to hide his secret feelings.

The chief nodded, and even Schonchin John
agreed. No, these two whites had never lied to the
Modocs, but they were only two among many.

"There are others," insisted Judge Roseborough.
"Some of them are waiting at Fairchild's ranch for
news of our talk. One is General Canby, who is now
chief of all the soldiers. The chief who led the battle on
the rocks has been sent away. Canby takes his place.
You will find him just, and his words are true. He does
not promise what he cannot carry out. Another who
waits is a minister, Reverend Thomas, and since he is
a man of God, you know he must speak only truth.
Then there is Colonel Meacham, the man who talked

91

to you on Lost River just before you went on the reservation the first time. You know he is a fair man. Mr. Fairchild will be there too. The Hot Creek Modocs will vouch for him. These are the men who are waiting to talk peace with you."

"The Modocs will talk," agreed Jack after conferring with the men on the inner circle. "But there must be no soldiers there with guns. And I will take an equal number of unarmed braves with me."

The meeting broke up, and Billy saw that much of the original anger of the tribesmen had gone. Some of them even spoke genially to the white men as they and Tobey prepared to mount their horses to return.

The first peace meeting was to be at Fairchild's ranch, and Captain Jack and his braves left early the next morning. He took with him Bogus Charley, Boston Charley, Hooker Jim and Dave Rock, and as the five men rode away Billy wondered why Schonchin John had not been included. Then he decided it must be because the chosen had the best understanding of the white man's tongue. Even though Tobey would be there to translate, it was wise to have a second pair of hearing ears. Someday, he told himself, he would be chosen for such a mission. He would rather do that than hide behind the rocks and take the lives of men.

He pulled the collar of his woolen shirt more closely about his throat as protection from a sudden gust of wind which blew straight from the snow mountains. Rabbit Ear Dave had given him the shirt, for the one he had worn when he arrived had grown too small. This one had been taken from the body of a volunteer, stripped of his clothing on the battlefield. At first Billy had felt strange wearing a garment of a dead man, but it was all he had and there was comfort in its warmth.

High overhead he heard the cries of geese, and when he looked up he could see the black V, like a pointed arrow, against the watery sky. He wished the flock would put down in Tule Lake. A meal of their rich flesh would make a welcome change. But the geese continued on, following their leader, and Billy gave up staring at them. Still, their arrival was a sign of coming spring, and there were other signs as well. The mule deer in the lava beds were moving restlessly, grazing farther and farther every day. The women had reported that early mullet were beginning to arrive in the lake to spawn. They had even managed to net a few and bring them back, but the rich, oily fish, usually so tender and white, were soft and yellow, strong to the taste and hardly edible. The hungry Modocs ate them anyway.

Billy hoped that the talks between Captain Jack and the whites would result in peace. Although the Stronghold had proved safe, it would be good to return to Lost River when springtime was upon them.

The chief did not bring back news of peace, only of a temporary truce. The white general, Canby, had proposed a series of talks, and to make it easier for both sides he wanted to set up a special Wa Wa Tent, or Talk Tent, midway between them. He was moving his own camps, one to the bottom of the bluffs, which brought it within a mile and a half of the Stronghold, the second camp to the peninsula north and across the lake. Meanwhile, he promised that none of the soldiers would fire on the Indians unless provoked, while the Modocs were free to come and go on the lake or lava beds as they pleased. Since the hunters had been creeping regularly to the grazing herds of mule deer and women had been daily visiting the lake after water, the last concession made the people laugh.

"But now we can visit the soldiers' camps," pointed out Bogus Charley craftily. "We can spy out their strength and perhaps bring back a few presents. The white man loves to make presents. It makes him feel superior."

Yes, the people agreed, that was so. The provision of the treaty was not so funny as it first appeared.

The following day the white tents high on the bluffs began to vanish, but soon they reappeared at the bottom. Now others besides Rabbit Ear Dave and the keen-eyed scouts could discern their trim, military lines that seemed to stretch on and on. Surely there must be a great many soldiers to need so large an encampment, and new reinforcements arrived almost every day.

One of these reinforcement parties came upon the herd of Modoc ponies, grazing in a protected place away from the Stronghold and drove the animals before them into the soldiers' camp. The Modocs were angry, and a party of women, headed by Princess Mary, Captain Jack's sister, and accompanied by Bogus Charley as interpreter, went to demand the return of the stolen animals.

General Canby refused. He and Colonel Meacham had an argument about the matter, reported Bogus. The colonel claimed that the theft had broken the truce, but Canby insisted no lives had been taken so the truce was intact. The ponies would be fed in military corrals on army food. When peace was arranged every pony would be returned.

"Treachery!" the Modocs cried. "Another of the white man's lies."

Still something good had come of the incident. The women had been sent since it was not deemed safe to trust the lives of fighting men so close to the headquarters of the soldiers. Both Bogus Charley and the women had been treated well. They had seen the guns and ammunition, the howitzers and cannon balls, the stacks of bayonets, which could be fitted onto the muzzles of the rifles. No one had stopped them from looking. In fact, many of the soldiers had talked with Bogus Charley, boasting of the great things they meant to do if the Modocs would not sign the treaty.

"I will go back," Bogus promised Jack. "I will take others with me. We will talk small and listen large. Many of the soldiers are stupid. They tell more than they think they are saying."

Bogus and Hooker Jim returned from the next visit to the camp with solemn faces. The soldiers had told them that their general had sent for a hundred Warm Springs warriors to act as scouts. The Warm Springs lived a hundred miles north of the Klamaths and Modocs and were ancient enemies of both tribes. Known as expert trackers and fierce warriors, their addition to the army was disquieting news. It was easy to fight and elude the whites, but Indian fighters were a different matter.

On the morning set for the first of the peace talks in the Wa Wa Tent, Captain Jack chose his men carefully. This time Dave Rock and Boston Charley were left behind and Schonchin John and Scar Face Charley took their places.

"Why not take Billy Modoc, too?" asked Scar Face. "He speaks the white man's tongue. He need not join the council, but if he listens to the talk of the soldiers guarding the tent, what he overhears may prove useful."

Billy held his breath. It was what he had hoped for all along, a chance to prove his worth.

Curly Headed Doctor jumped to his feet. He was angry that he himself had not been included in the peace talks.

"That one is yet a boy," he objected. "He has not made his quest."

"That is not his fault." To Billy's surprise, Bogus Charley came to his defense. He laughed, enjoying Curly Headed Doctor's discomfort. "At a time when every warrior is needed, why have you held him back? He has the size of a man and I myself have seen him shoot an arrow with great accuracy."

Curly Headed Doctor stalked away, unwilling to meet the questioning faces about him.

"Billy Modoc shall go," agreed Captain Jack. Then, turning to the boy, he added, "Listen well that you may report everything you hear. Ask questions, and remember what is said to you. We will set out at once."

It would have been more fitting if they could have arrived astride their wiry little ponies, but the ponies were gone. They had to travel the distance on foot.

Billy brought up the rear. Walking single file and just ahead of him were Bogus Charley and Hooker Jim. They were the two tallest men in the Modoc tribe, both over six feet, but Billy realized suddenly that he was almost as tall as they. Moreover, his shoulders were wide, and he was still growing. At least his mother said he was. Sometimes she looked anxiously at the wool shirt Rabbit Ear Dave had brought him from the battlefield and complained that by summer Billy would not be able to squeeze into it. But by summer he would not need it. The Modocs would be back on Lost River, rebuilding their village, and it would be too warm for any shirt.

The Wa Wa Tent was pitched in the open, with no protecting boulders close at hand. The general had chosen the position carefully, thinking that no one could approach it unseen. The warriors laughed as they guessed what he had done. The general did not know Modocs, they told each other.

There were a dozen soldiers standing around outside. They had no rifles. At least Billy could see none. At one side of the tent was a wagon, open at the back. A cook wagon, he recognized from his long association with the whites, and beside it a fire was burning on the ground.

When he saw the wagon, Hooker Jim turned and asked Billy about it.

"It is for food," he explained. "They plan to feed us."

Hooker Jim looked alarmed and spoke softly to Bogus Charley. Billy could see that his information about the refreshments was being passed along down the line. He knew what they were thinking. Ben Wright had invited the Modocs to a feast of friendship, then poisoned the food.

A man in a blue uniform, glittering with gold, came from the tent at their arrival. He was followed by a bearded officer in a uniform only a little less glittering, a third man in a dusty black suit with a preacher's collar and a fourth man in a business suit. Billy did not recognize any of them. In fact, he gave them only a brief glance, for coming from the cook wagon was a sound he had never thought to hear again.

"*Kwa, kwa, kwa!*"

It was the call of the female duck, and while ducks were familiar enough on Tule Lake, he had never expected to hear one in a cook wagon.

Chapter Ten

A MOMENT LATER A SMALL FIGURE, WEARING A TOO-
large army shirt and a pair of trousers hacked off
above his ankles, jumped from the wagon. His thin,
old-man face was split by a smile of welcome.

"Billy," he called joyfully. "Billy Morrison!"

Billy stood where he was, the pleasure of seeing
his old friend quenched by the sight of finding him
here. Bud was the enemy! On the trail to the tent he
had wondered if he would meet anyone he had known
at Linkville. Then he decided such a thing was impossible. The scouts had reported that the volunteer army
had gone home, leaving the campaign in the hands of
the military.

Bogus Charley pushed past Hooker Jim, and his
crafty face peered into Billy's.

"You know that boy?" he asked.

"Once he was my friend." He could see that Bud

was still waving and calling his name.

"Then he will feel free to talk with you." Bogus Charley's eyes bored hard into his. "He will have heard much, living in the soldier's camp. Learn everything he knows. Wave your hand as he is doing and call his name. Make him believe that everything between you is unchanged."

Hesitantly, Billy obeyed. It didn't seem right to take advantage of a friendship, but Bogus Charley must know best.

The white officers escorted Captain Jack and his party to the back of the cook wagon, where boxes of hardtack had been laid out. Hardtack was carried by the soldiers in the field, the general explained. It was a round white cracker, almost the consistency of a rock, but when it was dipped in water or coffee it could be bit into and was very nourishing.

Bud began passing out tin cups filled with the steaming black coffee that had been boiled on the fire. As he handed one to Billy, he gave a conspiratorial wink that seemed to say, "I'll see you later."

The Modocs accepted the tin cups and a round cracker, but no one put either to his lips.

"You and your men will have to eat first, General Canby," said a woman's voice. Tobey Riddle had come up behind them. Her husband, Frank, was by her side. "They remember when Ben Wright tried to poison their people."

Canby was the man with the most medals. Billy saw the startled look that the general gave Tobey, but he seemed to understand. He dipped his hardtack into his coffee cup, and after it had soaked a moment, he took a bite followed by a gulp of scalding coffee. The other whites immediately followed his example.

The Modocs waited a few moments and when there were no serious after effects, they too began to dip their crackers into their cups.

The coffee had already been sweetened with brown sugar, and so much had been added that Billy found it almost sickening. He didn't like the hardtack, either. Even after it had been soaked, it was difficult to chew. The Modocs, however, seemed to enjoy it, and when they joined the white men in the Wa Wa Tent some of their uneasiness was gone.

"Don't you have to go in, too?" asked Bud, when he saw that Billy hadn't followed the others.

"I'm not important enough to go to the council." He must be careful what he said. "I just came along to. . . . Well, I just came."

"Then it's got to be providence watching over us," declared Bud happily. "Every time I looked at them rocks I wondered if you was there and wished you'd come out. And here you are!"

"Here I am." Billy smiled at his friend. Somehow he couldn't think of Bud as the enemy. They had shared too much together. "I never figured to see you, though. By now I thought you'd have lit out for Frisco, the way you always said you would."

"Oh, I'm still going." Bud began gathering up discarded tin cups to rinse in a bucket of water. "I just been too busy. After you left, your pa hired me to help out in the stable. He couldn't do it alone, not with being deputy sheriff, and all. He was sure mad when you went, too."

Billy nodded. He hunkered down, Modoc fashion, with his knees folded and his bottom a few inches above the ground. That way the cold didn't penetrate his bones.

"Pretty soon his new son will be big enough to help out," he said.

"Son?" Bud laughed. "You're the only son he's got. His missus had a girl. Your pa was fit to be tied. I heard Sheriff McVey tell him better luck next time, and your pa 'lowed there wasn't going to be no next time."

For once Mrs. Etta's plans hadn't worked out to her satisfaction! It was hard to believe.

"How'd you get in the army?" he asked after a long minute.

"I'm not in the army exactly." Bud's tone was a little reluctant. "Course they pay me, and better'n your pa done, too. I get four dollars a month and my grub. I'm the cook's helper, and that means I do the dirty work that he don't like to do, like building fires and washing up. If I was older, they'd let me enlist and then I'd be a regular soldier. But this is almost as good, and I don't get shot at."

"Do you think the war will go on very long?" asked Billy cautiously. Bogus Charley had ordered him to ask questions, but Bogus Charley hadn't known his friend was just a cook's helper.

"Pshaw, no!" Bud spat contemptiously at a clump of nearby sagebrush. "Why, even if the peace talks don't come to nothing, we got a thousand men in our camp. And a hundred Warm Springs Indians on the way."

"You'd never take the Stronghold." Billy felt called upon to defend his own tribesmen.

"But we can smash it. We got cannon," Bud pointed out with a superior wave of his hand. "Howitzers. All kinds of big guns. We could shell you out in no time."

Billy remembered another of Bogus Charley's rules. Talk small and listen large. He did not comment on the cannon.

"When are the Warm Springs coming?" he asked instead.

"Any time now," Bud told him confidently. "We been looking for them for a couple of days. We won't do nothing till they get here. But the general says we won't need them if the peace talks work out. Say, you haven't told me about yourself. Did you have any trouble getting to your ma's people?"

"No trouble," Billy said briefly. He'd just as soon forget the details of that arduous trip. It had taken two weeks and he had lost his way more than once. Then he had trouble locating the Modoc's winter camp. When he finally found it he had been without food for two days and his bare toes were protruding from his worn-out shoes. Such an experience was better put from his mind.

Although he tried more questions, it was evident that Bud had told him all he knew of the soldiers' plans. He did say that both General Canby and Colonel Meacham were well liked by the men. The Reverend Thomas was a little pious for Bud's taste, but he meant well. Mr. Dyer, the Indian agent for the Klamath Reservation, was newly arrived, and as yet Bud had formed no opinion of him.

It was midafternoon before the initial peace talk broke up and the men emerged from the Wa Wa Tent. By the jutting angle of Schonchin John's jaw and the anger in his eyes, Billy could tell that it had not been successful. He said good-bye to Bud, and as the Modocs prepared to return to the Stronghold he took his place at the end of the line.

This time Scar Face Charley took the position just ahead of him.

"Did you hear anything?" He spoke over his shoulder when they were safely beyond the tent.

"They have a thousand soldiers," reported Billy.

"A thousand!" repeated Charley. "And we have fifty-six warriors. Anything else?"

"The hundred Warm Spring scouts are expected any day. Even if the peace talks fail, General Canby will not attack before they arrive."

"He is a wise man," decided Scar Face thoughtfully. "And a dangerous enemy. Many of the white chiefs are stupid, but not this one. They need those scouts. Only an Indian can think like another Indian."

Captain Jack made his report to the council of warriors that night, and from his place on the outer rim Billy listened eagerly. More than once during the afternoon he had looked at the nearby Wa Wa Tent and wondered what was happening inside. Afterwards, none of those present had given out so much as a hint. That was for their chief to do.

"The white man will not let us return to our home," Captain Jack told them flatly. "Since the blood of white settlers has been spilled on the Lost River, they say that to return is impossible. Feelings would be too strong between our people and the whites. It would result in further warfare."

For a moment the Modocs murmured angrily, then they were quiet as the chief continued.

"I asked if we could make our permanent home here in the lava beds. We know them like we know the lines in our hands, and with proper preparation we could winter here quite comfortably. No white settler would want this place. It would never serve his purpose. The white chief said no."

"Did you tell them we would never return to the land of the Klamaths?" shouted Curly Headed Doctor.

"Even that is barred from us now," said Captain Jack. "Many of the fighters in the battle on the rocks came from near the Klamath lands. The very name of Modoc brings fear to their hearts. They want to send us far away across the mountains to a country where our people are unknown."

Now there was no quelling the angry protests. This was their home. They had been here before the white man came. What the Modoc had done was only in defense of his own land. It was the white man who should be sent away.

"The white chief, General Canby, has a thousand soldiers at his command. He has stacks of guns and ammunition. He has cannon and cannon balls. One hundred Warm Springs scouts are on their way to help him. Soon we will be summoned to another peace talk, but I do not think the white man can be swayed."

Schonchin John jumped to his feet.

"I am an old man. I have listened to the lies of whites many times. Today I listened to more lies. I have no wish to be fooled again. I could read the hearts of the white men who spoke, and I know what they are doing by calling for more talks. They are stalling for time while they await the arrival of our old enemy, the Warm Springs. A hundred white soldiers are not worth one skilled Indian warrior. I would like to hear the opinion of some of our other fighting men."

A tall, dark-skinned Indian arose and jumped up on a rock which made him appear even taller. The people looked at each other in surprise. Black Jim, a fighter without fear, was usually silent at the councils.

He was Captain Jack's half-brother, but so far he had taken neither side in the arguments about the whites. That he was preparing to speak now was almost without precedent.

"Schonchin John speaks clearly and with wisdom," he said. "I also am tired of the white man's lies and treachery. I do not want to wait, like a duck floating on the lake, for the hunter's arrow. It is as easy to die tomorrow as it is a moon from now. Let us kill the white men who talk peace. Kill them now before the Warm Springs arrive. All who are of that mind, step to my side."

There was a great stirring among the warriors in the inner circle. Billy craned his neck to see better. Beside Black Jim stood Schonchin John, Boston Charley, Dave Rock, Shacknasty Jim, Little Steve, Ellen's Man, Bogus Charley, Curly Headed Doctor, Steamboat Frank, Hooker Jim and several others who were concealed from his view.

The other Indians had not moved from their places on the ground. Now one of them rose, and Billy saw that it was Weium, called Faithful William by the whites.

"I am a Modoc," said Weium calmly. "I am one of you. The way you decide this matter is not right. Black Jim is not our head chief. Captain Jack is our head chief. We must have his opinion before such a decision is reached."

Slowly Captain Jack arose.

"Like my half-brother, I am not afraid to die tomorrow or in the next moon," he announced. "But this is a serious thing you plan. It is a treacherous thing, for we are meeting under a white flag. Would the Modoc stoop to treachery?"

106

As he sat down, Scar Face Charley leaped to his feet.

"Today there was one peace talk. Who has heard of peace coming from a single talk? There must be many talks to reach an understanding. Each side must give a little in the end. You have seen the tents of the soldiers. Line after line of tents, enough for a thousand men. I am not afraid to die. You are not afraid to die. But why should we throw away our own and the lives of our children?"

His voice was drowned in the angry protests of Black Jim's supporters, and at last Scar Face Charley took his seat.

"Jack, you cannot save our people with your peace talks," cried Black Jim angrily. "Are you blind, my chief? A thousand soldiers are here already, and more are coming every day! The only way to get an even start on the peacemakers is to kill them at the next council. Without leaders, the soldiers cannot act."

Schonchin John stalked over to confront his chief.

"It is your duty to kill the head chief of the soldiers when we meet again. I will kill the second chief and there will be other warriors to kill the rest of the whites at the talk."

"That is a coward's act," began Jack, but his words were muffled for someone had thrown a woman's shawl around his shoulders. Someone else had picked up a basket and pushed it down over his head.

Billy caught his breath in disbelief. Captain Jack was their chief. He was acting in the best interests of his people. How dare they treat him so?

"Coward! Woman!" taunted Black Jim's followers. "We disown you. Sit there, you fish-hearted woman. You are not a Modoc."

Angrily, Jack snatched the basket from his head and shrugged off the shawl.

"I am neither a woman nor a coward," he cried, and his eyes defied them all. "But you would have me act like one. When Ben Wright asked our warriors to the feast, it was in the name of friendship. When they would not eat the poisoned food, the white men turned their guns upon our unarmed people. What you ask of me is the same. The Wa Wa Tent is a place where we strive for friendship and understanding. Honorable men should not break that truce."

"It is not the same!" shouted Black Jim. "When Ben Wright held his feast, we were not at war. Now we are. You have only to look at the lines of soldier tents, the big guns pointed at our Stronghold. If the whites had been able to penetrate the rocks, they would have slain every Modoc to the youngest child!"

"No, it is not the same!" Black Jim's words were echoed by all the warriors, and their angry faces told Billy that they would never be convinced.

As Captain Jack stared around the circle, he must have realized the same thing. The anger on his face gave way to something like sadness.

"I am your chief because you have made me so," he said finally. "You will not be guided by my words, but you are my people and I must do your will though it costs me my life and the lives of many others. It is the act of a coward, but I will do it because you ask it of me."

Without glancing at either side, he stalked to his cave in the lava rocks. Left behind, Black Jim and his followers danced the war dance until dawn.

Chapter Eleven

"IT WOULD BE WELL IF YOU WERE AGAIN SENT TO THE Wa Wa Tent," said Billy's mother. "I have used all the hardtack you brought back and perhaps your friend would give you more. Chipmunk is chewing on the last piece. It eases the pain of the new teeth coming in."

"I will not be sent again," Billy told his mother honestly. "The news I brought was of little worth. Bogus Charley had found out everything I did."

He looked at his little brother, gumming happily on the round, hard cracker and wished he had brought more. Bud had loaded his pockets with soldier's rations before he left. Billy hadn't really wanted them, but was too polite to say so. Sally, on the other hand, received them with joy. She set aside a few for Chipmunk, and the remainder she pounded to a powder on rocks. Mixed with dried beef, the hardtack baked into cakes that even Billy admitted were quite tasty and a change from their monotonous diet.

It had been several days since the first peace talk, and there was still no summons to the second. Each morning Rabbit Ear Dave and the other scouts watched the roads for the arrival of the Warm Springs, while Bogus Charley, Hooker Jim and Boston Charley boldly ventured into the soldiers' camp. They were well received, and the Sunday Preacher, the Reverend Thomas, had even given Bogus and Boston several pieces of clothing.

Billy left his mother hurriedly as someone shouted that a rider was approaching the Stronghold. It proved to be Tobey Riddle bearing the message that the second peace talk would be held the following day. Schonchin John and his followers were especially cordial to her, and Billy knew it was because they were pleased that now their plan to kill the peacemakers could be carried out.

"Have you heard of the great honor which has been given to me?" Ellen's Man asked as they watched the Indian woman ride away again.

Billy shook his head. He had not been invited to the meetings where details of the plan were discussed. For once he was glad to be excluded. It was not right to do this thing.

"I am to be behind Captain Jack himself when the moment comes to kill the big chief of the whites," Ellen's Man told him proudly. "If our chief falters, or his gun should fail, I will be there to take his place. The honor will be mine."

Billy stared at the boy, scarcely older than himself. Ellen's Man's eyes glowed with a strange light that he had never seen before. He felt a sudden chill come over him.

"You could really do it?" he asked. "Just walk up to a man and shoot him in the breast?"

"Of course," agreed Ellen's Man. "He is our enemy." Then, because he was enjoying the amazement on Billy's face, he continued. "It is all arranged. Schonchin John will kill the second chief, the one called Old Man Meacham. Shacknasty Jim will be at his side to help him. The Sunday Doctor will be slain by Bogus Charley and Boston Charley. He will suspect nothing. Did he not give them new shirts just the other day? Black Jim and Hooker Jim will take care of the agent from Klamath Reservation. Black Jim is not happy, because that one is the least important. But he is all that is left except for Kaitch-ka-na and her white husband."

"You can't kill her. She's a Modoc," protested Billy.

"No longer!" For a moment the smile faded from the brown face, and Ellen's Man frowned fiercely. "There is a traitor in our tribe. Someone told Kaitch-ka-na of our plan, and she warned the white soldiers."

"Who? How?"

"No one knows." Ellen's Man shrugged. "But it does not matter. The stupid soldiers did not believe her. When Bogus Charley went to their camp yesterday, the Sunday Preacher asked him about it. Bogus said it was a lie, and Sunday Preacher believed him, not Kaitch-ka-na. That is why he gave Bogus the extra shirt."

"But to kill Tobey—Kaitch-ka-na. . . . If she told, she was only doing what she thought was right."

"She will not be killed," admitted Ellen's Man regretfully. "When he heard, Scar Face Charley said he would hide in the sagebrush nearby and his rifle would pick off anyone who harmed her. He would do it, too, so that part of the plan was forgotten. The two-tongued woman will live a little longer."

Billy breathed more easily. At least Tobey was safe. No one would challenge Scar Face Charley's marksmanship. And the whites had been warned. Perhaps they were not all so gullible as Sunday Preacher.

"They'll never let you near the Wa Wa Tent with rifles," he pointed out reasonably. "Even if they didn't believe Kaitch-ka-na, they will be watching."

"There will be rifles if we need them," Ellen's Man told him. "Tonight, when it is dark, Boncho and Slolux will carry many rifles and hide behind the sagebrush only a little way from the Wa Wa Tent. But we will not need rifles until we leave, and then only for the soldiers who may pursue us. We will have pistols hidden in our shirts. Close at hand, we cannot miss."

"No," agreed Billy soberly. "I don't see how you can."

Later that evening, while the warriors who would take part in the massacre were gathered around Curly Headed Doctor's fire, he sought out Scar Face Charley.

"Can't you stop it?" he asked.

"No." Charley looked across to where Curly Headed Doctor was making special medicine for to-morrow. "The blood of our people runs as hot as the sun in summer. Words will not stop them now. I can only save Kaitch-ka-na."

During the night, the two warriors, Boncho and Slolux, loaded down with rifles, stole out of the rocks and crept across the lava beds. Billy did not envy them their long wait hidden in the sagebrush. For hour after hour they must lie there, scarcely daring to move a muscle, waiting for a sign that they were needed.

At daybreak, the party of Modocs chosen for the peace talk started out. Led by Captain Jack, who walked proudly lest someone should again accuse him of cowardice, the others followed, Schonchin John, Bogus and Boston Charley, Black Jim, Shacknasty and Hooker Jim and Ellen's Man. Except for Ellen's Man, who was smiling as though his mouth might split at either corner, all were grim-eyed, and their faces were stern. They carried no visible arms, but Billy knew that pistols were concealed beneath their shirts.

Fifty yards behind them stalked Scar Face Charley, with his rifle prominently displayed. He had made sure that the others saw it before he left, and while he would be hidden in the sagebrush they also knew that he would be within firing range.

Billy's empty stomach seemed to writhe and churn as he watched them go down the trail beside the lake. He was still watching when he saw Curly Headed Doctor and Curly Headed Jack, one of the young warriors whom he knew only slightly, leave the Stronghold. They did not follow the trail to the Wa Wa Tent but struck out in a southeastern direction across the lava beds. Since they carried rifles, he concluded they were after game and forgot about it.

The hours seemed to go on forever. The warriors left behind gathered on the ledge under the medicine flag. They spoke quietly, if at all. Younger children went about their usual play. Women carried on their daily tasks, gathering sagebrush for the fires and caring for babies in the cradle boards. They went to the lake for water and some brought back a few spawned-out mullet for food. Flocks of ducks and geese were daily lighting on the lake after their winter's migration south, but no hunter went after them today. This was like no other day. It was a day when the fate of the Modocs would be decided.

When the sun had nearly reached the top of its climb, there seemed to be a disturbance about the tent. Even from this distance, Modoc ears caught the faint sounds of gunshots.

"I can see them," announced Rabbit Ear Dave. "The soldier guards are alarmed. They run here and there, like ants."

"What else? What else do you see?" A dozen anxious voices clamored for news.

"One of the ants is running away. There is much confusion." Dave kept his eyes at the peephole in the rocks. "Our men are coming back. They are running this way."

"All of them?"

"I cannot tell."

But soon everyone could see for himself. Loping easily over the rough lava, the Modoc warriors were returning to the Stronghold. Each man had stopped long enough to secure a rifle from the pile that Boncho and Slolux had waiting for them, but the rifles were not needed. The soldiers were not in pursuit. Before long the party was ascending the winding incline to the Stronghold.

"I have done what you asked of me," Captain Jack told the people. His voice was cold, without expression. "The first chief of the soldiers is dead." With that he turned and disappeared into his own cave.

The other warriors were not so scanty in their

details. Schonchin John had killed Old Man Meacham. At least he was almost positive he had, but when he tried to take his scalp Kaitch-ka-na, who had thrown herself over the colonel's fallen body, had shouted an alarm.

"The soldiers are coming!" she cried.

When they heard that, the Modocs did not wait. They left the now bloody Wa Wa Tent to return to the Stronghold.

Bogus and Boston Charley were sure that Sunday Doctor was dead, but Black Jim and Hooker Jim had to report that the agent Dyer had escaped. Black Jim's gun had jammed, and before Hooker could raise his own, the white man slid out the tent flaps and was bounding toward the camp at the foot of the bluffs. They had fired after him, but the man stumbled so over rocks that it was impossible to take accurate aim.

The standbys for the actual killers had not been idle either. Although it had not been necessary for them to fire a shot, they had rushed forward and stripped the slain men of their clothing. Ellen's Man carried General Canby's many-medaled coat and hat, Shacknasty Jim had Colonel Meacham's, while Boston Charley displayed the black coat and white shirt with its strange collar that had belonged to Sunday Preacher.

Billy turned away from the heap of clothing and sickness rolled about in his stomach. The garments were stained with scarlet around the powder burns. He hoped that some of the women would wash them before he had to look again.

Later that afternoon, Curly Headed Doctor and Curly Headed Jack returned. On being pressed, they admitted sheepishly that they had undertaken an un-

115

successful mission of their own. They had tried to lure the white leader of the second soldier camp into the open, but the man had proved too wily. They were lucky to escape with their lives.

The Modocs laughed heartily at their discomfort, and Curly Headed Doctor stalked indignantly away.

Scar Face Charley had returned, too, but he did not take part in the celebration of the others. He stood apart, leaning on his rifle, and his face looked grave.

"Did anyone try to kill Kaitch-ka-na?" Billy came over to stand by him.

"No." Scar Face shook his head. "Boncho tried to steal her horse, but when I called to him he let it go." He turned to look deep into the boy's eyes. "It is a sad day for the Modocs, Billy," Scar Face told him. "You should have stayed with your father's people."

The attack on the Stronghold began three days later. Billy wondered why the army did not attack at once, but Scar Face told him they had probably sent for a new general. With Canby and Meacham both dead, the younger officers were afraid to act on their own.

On that morning, just as the first rim of sun appeared above the mountains, the Modoc guards on the ledge reported a movement of troops in the camp below the bluffs. Gradually they sorted themselves out and a long line of fighting men advanced upon the Stronghold. There was no fog today to hide behind and in full view the men marched toward them.

The Modocs were waiting, each behind his assigned peephole, his rifle in position. When the soldiers arrived within firing range, the volley sounded. As the smoke cleared, Bill could see half a dozen motionless forms sprawled on the rough ground, but that was the end. The soldiers retreated just beyond range and sat down to wait. They waited all day, a long line of blue which gave off an occasional glint as the sun picked up the shine of metal.

The Modocs waited too. There was no sense in wasting valuable ammunition on men who were out of range, but at nightfall the sentinels on the ledge were doubled. The hunters dared not go out for food, but some of the women who bravely ventured to the lake for water were not fired upon.

The sentinels reported movement in the lava beds during the night and kept their rifles ready, but with the enemy so close no scouts went out. By morning light the Modocs could see a line of breastwork made of lava boulders piled up within firing range. How the soldiers had managed so quietly in the darkness they couldn't imagine. Perhaps a wind which had sprung up during the night had blown the sounds away.

The battle was resumed at once, but as before the soldier's bullets bounced harmlessly off the rocks, The Modocs had no way of knowing whether their own rifles found a mark.

Their water supply was growing low, and the women who tried to go to the lake now for more were fired upon. They hoarded what water they had, making it go as far as possible. Billy told his mother to give Chipmunk most of his share. He himself sucked on a rock. It made the juices of his mouth flow a little and he could almost forget that he was thirsty.

After three days of the siege the white soldiers hauled their big guns to a position behind the Stronghold. Soon cannon balls were pounding on the rock. The roar was deafening and no one could hear another speak. It went on and on. But Bud had been wrong

117

when he said the cannon would destroy the fortress. The rocks held.

Captain Jack gave the order to fire only when a direct target was in range. The soldiers were aiming at the holes from which issued the smoke of Modoc rifles. Without these signs the cannon balls and rifles had no target. Still the soldiers continued their attack, firing blindly. Unlike the Modocs they had plenty of ammunition.

The women and children had all been ordered into the caves, which gave the greatest protection of all. Billy did not consider himself a child, but he dared remain no longer at the peephole on the ledge. Someone, probably Curly Headed Doctor, might order him away.

He went below, to the level place where the Modocs held their councils. Two young braves were there before him, and Billy wondered why they had left their places on the ledge. One was Shacknasty Jim's younger brother, George, and the other was called Eddie. Although they were close to Billy's age, he did not know them well. Most of the boys, like Pete Schonchin, who had only made their quest for power last year, were friendly enough, but George and Eddie had always ignored him completely.

Usually he avoided them, but today curiosity drew him close.

"Where did you get that?" He spoke without thinking.

They were trying to pry open a huge shell which had soared over the breastworks and tumbled into the crater below.

"It is ours," said Eddie quickly. "We found it. It is a big soldier bullet."

"It's from a howitzer." Billy had seen one once in Linkville. "You had better leave it alone. It could go off."

"This one is dead," George announced positively. "We are going to open it and see what is inside."

His mother, Shacknasty Liz, appeared in the doorway of her cave and screamed at him to leave the thing alone. He might get hurt.

George and Eddie exchanged amused glances. What did a woman know of such things?

"I will get an axe," volunteered Eddie, jumping to his feet. "We will have to smash it open."

"Don't," protested Billy. "Your mother is right. It is full of gunpowder."

"Listen to the boy who has not even made a quest," taunted George. "Run to the caves with the women, boy, if you are afraid."

Billy hesitated a moment, but when Eddie returned with a heavy stone axe, and George began hollowing a depression in the ground to hold the shell steady, he followed their advice. He ran for the cave, shouting as he went.

"Stay inside! Everyone stay far back in your caves."

His mother was sitting on the ground, trying to quiet Chipmunk who was terrified by the constant shelling. She had not heard his alarm, for she had stuffed bits of cloth in her own and Chipmunk's ears in an effort to muffle the sound. But she saw the great flash of light from the council place outside the cave. She held Chipmunk close, protecting his small body with her own.

Billy waited a moment before he stepped to the entrance. The council ground still echoed from the noise of the exploding shell and the enclosure was filled with smoke. He could see a blackened spot on the ground where George had chopped a hollow to hold the shell, but there was no sign of either him or Eddie.

They were the first two Modoc casualties of the war.

Chapter Twelve

ALL NIGHT LONG THE FIRING CONTINUED. IT WAS NOT so constant, but there was enough to keep the Modoc women in their caves awake. On the ledge, the warriors were also awake. They dared not leave their posts. Hour after hour their eyes strained through the starlit darkness lest a raiding party attack the Stronghold.

Billy ventured to the ledge, and his own eyes were keen enough to pick out dark mounds scattered on the ground. Mule teams, dragging wagons, came into the field to gather up the dead, but Jack gave the order not to fire on the drivers. They were civilians, not soldiers, and despite their white skins their task was a sacred thing.

Hooker Jim and a small party disobeyed that order, but Billy did not hear of it until much later. Hooker had led a few warriors through a narrow crack in the south wall of the Stronghold. He had hoped to bring back needed ammunition by attacking the white's camp below the bluffs while the main party of soldiers was in the field. He had been discovered, and his warriors fired upon, but in the darkness no Modoc had been hurt. Angry at the failure of his scheme, Hooker Jim had killed a young driver of a mule team. He brought back the scalp as retribution.

At daybreak the firing of the cannon and the infantry resumed with the intensity of the day before. Billy followed the example of his mother and stuffed rags into his ears. He wondered if he would ever hear normally again. He had slept only a little in the cave, but the warriors on the ledge had rested even less. He found Scar Face Charley and asked diffidently if he couldn't relieve him for awhile.

"I have a rifle," he reminded the older man. "You gave it to me." He pulled a bit of rag from his ear as he awaited the reply.

"Do you have any bullets?" The long scar down Charley's cheek was even more evident this morning, and there were circles of weariness beneath his eyes. "Have you ever fired a gun?"

"No." The answer was the same for both questions.

"Then you must put the thought away," Charley told him. "Every shot must count. One bullet, one soldier. If we get out of here, I will find some bullets and teach you how to fire that gun, but not now. What you can do is to bring me some water."

"There is none," Billy told him sadly. It had rained two nights before and every container had been placed in position to catch the precious drops. "The women say they have searched every hollow in the rocks where sometimes rainwater is held. It is all gone."

Scar Face Charley nodded and turned his eyes back to the peephole in the rocks.

By midmorning, the early mist was gone and the sun shone in a cloudless sky. Truly, spring had come. With the air so filled with the smell of gunpowder, Billy could not smell the spring freshness, but he saw it in the vivid color of the grass covering the lava around the Stronghold. Even the sage had revived after its winter's rest, and now when the women threw it on the fires there was smoke as well as flame. Only a few of the usual thousands of water fowl still fished night and morning on Tule Lake. Alarmed by the noise of the battle, most of them had flown farther north to take up residence there. The Klamaths would rejoice, he thought resentfully.

With the rag stuffed in his ears, he had missed much of the conversation going on around him so he was surprised when he saw two women start down the winding incline to the lake. Both wore shawls across their heads, and each carried canteens, captured from the soldiers. The first woman he recognized by her perpetually stooped shoulders. She was very old and walked with a painful limp. The second was unknown to him, for her face was hidden by her shawl. But she also must have been among the older members of the tribe, for she, too, moved in a halting fashion.

Billy pulled the rag from one of his ears again, and spoke to the warrior nearest him on the ledge.

"What are the old ones going to do?" he asked incredulously.

"Get water if they can." The warrior turned, and beneath the grime, Billy could see that it was Pete Schonchin.

"They will be killed," he protested.

"Maybe," Pete admitted. "That is old Mary. She says death would relieve her of the aching in her bones. The devil within her gives her no peace, day or night. The one who follows is Lazy Luther."

"Lazy Luther? But he's no woman!"

"He says that when he returns with water, the people must change his name." White teeth flashed in Pete's dirty face. "He says we must call him Brave Luther, and he has the promise of the chief."

Billy had seen Lazy Luther about the camp and thought the name well given. He was always the last to respond to any call, and much preferred letting his younger brother bring home food for the family and take over the men's work. He was surprised that Lazy Luther had volunteered for such a mission.

"Will the soldiers let them through?" he asked wonderingly.

"Sometimes the whites are moved by pity for the very old," Pete told him. "It is our only chance."

Billy knew that was the truth. Only the night before, a group of warriors, with sagebrush tied to their backs for concealment, had tried to bring water from the lake. They had been discovered and driven back by the Springfield rifles of the soldiers.

He found a peephole in the rocks and applied his eye to it. Soon he could see old Mary hobbling along, bent almost double, as she made her way toward the lake. Behind her followed the second figure, muffled in a shawl, and also bent.

For a time the soldiers held their fire, then rifles

opened up. As they neared the lake, Lazy Luther forgot himself and straightened to his full height. The next moment he staggered and fell to the ground, while Old Mary dropped her canteens and began hobbling back to the Stronghold. She was allowed to reach it safely, but without water.

Before long the howitzers stopped their bombardment. Slowly, almost inch by inch, the two armies had closed in, forming a united line at the front. It was no longer possible to use cannon without firing on the foot soldiers. Although the Modocs were relieved to be rid of the echoing thunder against the rock walls and the flying fragments of stone, there was a new danger. Rabbit Ear Dave and some of the others had caught glimpses of Indians among the troops. The long-awaited Warm Springs had arrived.

That afternoon an attempt was made to storm the Stronghold. A soldier, wearing the uniform of an officer, mounted a boulder not more than twenty feet from the entrance. His company had been crawling through the lava field and now were lying in a gully just behind him.

"Come on, boys. Let's rush them!" shouted the officer. He was so close that Billy could distinguish every word.

Each Modoc drew a bead and fired, but miraculously, the officer still stood, waving his sword and calling to his men.

As the soldiers followed his order, they were picked off one by one, but the officer stood unharmed. Finally he jumped off the rock and out of view of the now thoroughly frightened Modoc warriors.

"He is a spirit soldier," said Hooker Jim in an awed tone. "I took good aim. No bullet could touch that one. I cannot fight a spirit."

"Perhaps it is an omen," suggested Little Ike.

"He is but one," growled Black Jim, but even his voice was a little nervous. "Look at the dead soldiers lying on the ground where he stood. They were not spirits."

Still, everyone knew that the situation was serious. Although the Modocs had lost but three warriors since coming to the Stronghold, and the losses of the whites were too many to count, they could hold out only a little longer. They were without water. Their only food was a little dried beef, and their ammunition was very low.

Leaving a few warriors on the ledge to return the gunfire of the enemy, the others retreated to the council place to make their plans.

"Let the people speak," said Captain Jack. "This war is yours. I did not seek it, but as your chief I must do your bidding."

"We must leave the Stronghold," cried Scar Face Charley. "I do not like to run, but it is the only thing left for us. Our women and children are in danger, as well as ourselves."

Jack waited a moment, but no one rose to dispute the suggestion.

"We will go south tonight," he agreed. "A party of young men, without wives, will make a great disturbance on the north side of the Stronghold. It will distract the soldiers while the others escape through the narrow crack in the rocks toward the south. Each man must be responsible for the safety of his own family. But if we are detected, then we will join together to make a stand. The lava beds are filled with giant rocks all known to you, and there are caves in many rocks for the women and children to hide in. When the last family is safely away, the young men will follow."

Billy listened eagerly while the names of the young men were called out. Even though he was not yet a warrior, he could make as loud a noise as anyone. But again he was passed over.

When Rabbit Ear Dave conducted Sally, Chipmunk and Deaf Tom through the narrow crack in the south wall, Billy went with them. Once, as he crawled through the darkened lava beds, he paused to look back over his shoulder.

The Stronghold loomed huge and black and jagged against the star-sprinkled sky, and the medicine flag still hung from the highest crag. Only three old Modocs, too sick and lame to travel, had been left behind. When the soldiers found them tomorrow, Billy hoped they wouldn't be harmed.

Chapter Thirteen

"ON THIS DAY I WILL TEACH YOU TO SHOOT THE WHITE man's gun," said Scar Face Charley.

Billy, who had been sitting on the ground, tossing a pebble in the air and catching it again for Chipmunk's delighted amusement, looked up in surprise.

"Do we have enough bullets?" he asked.

"Some," replied Scar Face gravely. "But we need more. That is why we must seek some bullets today."

The Modocs were encamped not too far from their former base. The anger against the white soldiers was very strong. Scouts had reported that the three old people left behind in the Stronghold had been ruthlessly killed. There had been several encounters with patrols, even some attacks upon small encampments. In each the Modocs had been successful. They had brought back many rounds of needed ammunition.

Billy jumped to his feet and ran to get the rifle

Scar Face had given him. Finally, he thought, he was to be allowed to take part in the battles.

There were fifteen men in the raiding party that Scar Face motioned Billy to join, with Billy bringing up the rear. Clutching his empty gun, Billy told himself that he made sixteen for he did not intend the rifle to remain empty long.

They set out single file on a trail that wound above the lower basin of the lava beds. On their left were jagged cliffs with a towering peak behind. It had proved useful to the Modocs when they first came. The rocky monolith was studded with many ice caves, caverns so deep and well protected that the ice never melted even on the warmest day. It had provided the tribe with needed drinking water. Below them on the right was an eerie thing to see. It was as though Ka-moo-cum-chux, who made this place, had grown tired and left his work undone, for a wide expanse of black lava cut through the green stubble of growth. A man could find footholds over the remainder of the lava beds, but not across this stretch. Even the scant vegetation which had found crevices of soil elsewhere for its shallow roots could find none here. The solid lava wound away like a dark, wide ribbon of needle-sharp rock, and to walk from one side of it to the other was impossible.

Suddenly, Scar Face Charley, who had been leading, held up his hand. Each warrior, alert always for danger, stopped, and at a second signal found himself a hiding place along the trail. Billy scrambled after them, falling to his knees behind a jagged boulder.

At first he heard nothing. Then it was as though his closed ears had been opened, for the jangle of metal upon metal, the shuffling sounds of feet became very audible. He could hear men's voices coming from the level below the rim.

Scar Face crawled forward, his long legs, wrapped in their bindings of rawhide for protection against the cuts of sharp stone, making no sound on the rocky trail. Cautiously he peered over, then he turned and to Billy's surprise, motioned the boy was to join him at the edge.

Billy followed. He was pleased that no pebble turned beneath him and that his progress was as silent as the older man's. All that training had been worthwhile.

"They make white man's talk." Scar Face Charley's whisper was so low that Billy could scarcely make it out. "Tell me what they say."

Billy inched forward, peering cautiously over the ledge. Below him was a scouting party of soldiers who had paused to rest. They were sitting on the rocky ground, ruefully surveying the wide streak of black, forbidding lava which they had chanced on unsuspectingly, and breaking out their noon rations as they talked. Billy had counted up to seventy men when Scar Face pulled him back, but he could still hear some of their conversation.

"Wish them Warm Springs would catch up." The man who spoke had a penetrating voice that carried on the clear air.

Billy could not make out the lower-voiced reply and was glad when the first man spoke again.

"It's a blame fool idea leaving them to guard that heap of rocks. The Modocs won't go back there, and we could use them Injun scouts here. Better than us wearing out our own feet. My corns is terrible."

Billy leaned forward again. He had a brief

glimpse of the speaker who was now removing his shoes. In that same instant he sensed that other men were doing the same.

"There's nary a Modoc around here." This was a new voice, but as carrying as the first. "Sort of wish we would run into a few. I'd like to get me one."

"When you don't see any Indians is just the time to look for them." This voice was sharp with authority, and Billy decided it might be the officer in charge. "I'm going to scout and see what's over that ridge. Who's with me?"

"A scouting party is coming up the slope," whispered Billy. He felt his heart pounding and wished that there were bullets in his gun.

Scar Face nodded grimly, then motioned to his warriors. Carefully, silently, they crawled forward to join him.

From below came the noise of heavy shoes clumsily trying to scale the cliff. Charley did not need anyone to interpret that. With a whoop, he leaned over the edge and his warriors did the same. Billy's nose was filled with the now familiar smell of gunpowder, and his ears tingled with the staccato charges of rifles, the war whoops of the braves beside him, and the terrified shouts of the men below.

"They've found some place to hide," called one of the warriors down the line.

"We will go down," decided Scar Face. "They will be in some fissure of the cliff."

As surefooted as wild goats, the Modocs descended the ledge and Billy followed a little more slowly. On the way he passed the bodies of the small group of soldiers who had attempted the climb. All were dead. There were dead and wounded soldiers on the field below, also, but the majority had taken refuge, as Scar Face had guessed, in a crevice in the slope. They attempted to defend themselves, but it was no use.

Billy turned away from the scene, and once more his stomach almost betrayed him. It took a great effort to retain what he had eaten earlier. As soon as he was calmer, he walked over to the pile where rifles had been stacked and began loading them into his arms. He took a great while about it.

"That is a smart thing to do." Scar Face Charley's voice sounded close to his ear, and for the moment Billy could not bring himself to look at the man. He kept on picking up rifles and slinging ammunition belts over his shoulders.

Scar Face called to his warriors, then slowly, as though thinking out each word at a time, he delivered a final message to any survivors on the battlefield.

"All you mans what ain't dead better go home," he shouted. "We don't want to kill you all in one day."

Now that the Modocs were again well supplied with ammunition, Scar Face gave Billy a lesson in marksmanship. It wasn't part of a battle, and there were just the two of them present. Curly Headed Doctor had been very angry when he found that a boy without power had accompanied the warriors on a raid. He threatened to put a curse on both of them if it happened again, and Scar Face told Billy it would be better not to take chances. But there was no harm in him learning to use a rifle if he only shot at targets.

Billy was secretly relieved. He wasn't sure he would be able to take part in a bloody massacre. But maybe Curly Headed Doctor was right. Once he had made a quest and received his spiritual power, he might feel differently.

There were several skirmishes after this which Billy did not see but only heard about. One was with a cavalry unit, and Captain Jack, dressed in General Canby's full regalia, taunted the soldiers from a ridge. It ended in a rout in which the cavalry drove the Indians into juniper thickets where horses could not follow. This time the Modocs were not so lucky. They lost a warrior, Little Stephen, but there was satisfaction in knowing that the horse soldiers could count several dead and wounded.

The last battle—the one they had been waiting for—was an encounter with the Warm Springs.

Scouts brought back news that the entire party of enemy Warm Springs, accompanied by a small detachment of cavalry, had trailed the Modocs to their camp. They were approaching rapidly and were then no more than a mile and a half away.

Captain Jack ordered the women and children to take cover in the rocks and sagebrush, while he led his warriors out to meet the advancing forces. This battle would be the kind of fighting they were used to, tribe against tribe, as their fathers had fought before them.

Billy was expected to go with the women, but he held back. This time, he told himself, his stomach would not betray him. Although he still lacked skill with the rifle, maybe he would be lucky.

"Curly Headed Doctor will put a curse on you if you try to join the warriors," warned his mother anxiously.

The medicine man, his painted face distorted with suspicion, was standing on the fringe of departing braves. His narrowed eyes were watching Billy carefully. After a moment, the boy gave up and put down his rifle. A curse was nothing to be taken lightly.

Angrily, he turned and followed his mother, who was bent under the growing weight of Chipmunk on her back.

From their hiding place in the juniper thicket they could hear the sounds of battle. The Modocs must have met the Warm Springs midway, and the fighting was taking place less than a mile distant. The discharge of rifles, the occasional neighing of a cavalry mount, the war whoops of both tribes were carried by a soft wind that stirred the grasses all about them. They knew that the Warm Springs, like the Modocs, would be shooting from behind boulders, grabbing bunches of sagebrush for concealment as they moved to more strategic sites. They would not be like the foolish soldiers who took their stand in the open, waiting to be picked off singly. Moreover, they were very evenly matched in numbers, for Modoc scouts had reported that the number of Warm Spring scouts to arrive fell short of the expected one hundred.

The battle went on for several hours while Billy and the women listened tensely. Then everything was silent.

"It is over," said an old woman near him. She had waited through many similar encounters. "Soon our men will return."

"Did we win?" Billy asked anxiously, wondering how she could be so assured.

"No one won," she answered. "The sounds did not grow distant, so our warriors did not pursue their enemy. Nor do they draw near, so our men are not pursued."

Billy did not see how this could happen, but he didn't say so. There had to be a winner and a loser in every battle. He hoped it was just a change in the wind that had carried the sounds away from them.

But the words of the old woman proved true. After a long wait, the warriors returned, their grimy faces set in stern lines. No one had won the battle. Both sides withdrew, but not as losers. It was a draw, and as was the custom in such cases the Indians stopped fighting. The cavalry had taken no part in the encounter. They had remained to one side, each man on his horse, leaving the tribes to fight alone.

But the Modocs had suffered one disastrous loss. They carried the body of a slain warrior, and that man was one who had gained the friendship of everyone. He was Ellen's Man.

On seeing this, the women set up a mighty keening. With tears running down their faces, some of them hurried to fetch pitch from the trees to rub in their hair as a sign of mourning.

Billy stared down at the motionless body on the ground. He felt a great emptiness within him and wished that he were like the women, free to show his grief in tears. Ellen's Man had tried to be a friend to all, even to a boy who had no power. There was something strange about the still face, so young that no hair grew upon it. At first Billy could not think what it could be, and then he knew. For the first time since he had joined the forces in the Stronghold, the face of Ellen's Man was without a smile.

"He died a hero's death," declared Captain Jack. "When we found him, there was a dead Warm Springs warrior on either side."

The Hot Creek warriors had gathered in a little group, talking in low voices, glancing occasionally at the still figure on the ground. Billy knew what they were thinking. Now that Ellen's Man was dead, his special power was gone. They could no longer depend on it for safety in battle. Some of the Lost River Modocs must have remembered, too, for their faces were as fearful as the Hot Creeks'.

"He never should have died," cried Black Jim. He stopped his angry pacing to pause before the chief. "We never should have gone out to meet the Warm Springs."

"Would you have had us await them here? Or run from them?" asked Jack. "Modocs have never run from the enemy."

"We should have hidden in ambush and attacked them when they least expected it. Had I been chief that would have been my plan." The cords in Jim's throat swelled and stood out like the wrapped strands of basket weaving.

"Perhaps you would like to take my place as chief?" Jack's round eyes narrowed and he stared up at his taller half-brother unafraid.

"Maybe it is a good idea," agreed Black Jim. "Ellen's Man might be alive if I were. As it is now, the enemy will follow us and pick us off one by one."

Billy could hardly believe what he was hearing. The Modocs began taking sides. Even the women, who were usually silent on such matters, added their voices to the tumult. The death of a favorite warrior was an excuse to vent their feelings. They had endured so much. For almost six months they had been fighting, then fleeing from their enemy. They had lost their home and were nearly starving. Moving camp regularly, as they were doing, the roots gathered by the women had been scanty and there had been little time for the hunters to bring in sufficient game. It was a relief now to take their anger out on something.

"Hear me!" Scar Face Charley's voice rose above the noise and for a few minutes everyone was silent. "We are not beaten. The white man has not whipped the Modoc, but a wise man knows when to stop. If we go in now under a white flag, we will need to run no longer. Our stomachs will be filled. It is not defeat if we stop fighting. We have proved our worth, and we cannot run forever."

Billy thought it was a sensible solution to the problem, but he was the only one. It was not what the others wanted to hear and the quarreling began anew.

Black Jim shook his fist at Captain Jack.

"You are not my chief," he shouted. "I will follow you no longer."

Captain Jack's contemptuous eyes stared back at him.

"And you are no longer my half-brother," he declared. "You are a yellow dog and show it by your words. Why do you come to me in anger because a man is killed? You must have known there would be many deaths among our people when, after the battle on the Lost River, you went with Hooker Jim and the other braves, following the white settlers to their homes and killing them there. I wanted peace, but you would not listen. You put a woman's basket on my head and called me coward. You made me kill the white officer. Now there can be no peace. As long as everything is good you are brave, but when dark clouds come you say that I am to blame."

"Kill him," shouted Bogus Charley. "He is not fit to lead us."

"You shall not kill him!" Weium threw his thin

body in front of the chief, but Captain Jack pushed Weium to one side and his voice rose clear and fearless.

"I am the one you have chosen to lead you. My way was the way of peace, but you chose instead to do battle with the white man. In battles, men must fall on either side. It has always been so. In the Stronghold, the Modocs lost few warriors, but we could not stay there. Now we must flee, with the white man snapping at our heels like vicious dogs. Our only hope is to wear them out. It has become a test of endurance, and in that time other men will die. I myself expect to die, but I would rather die in battle than at the end of the white man's rope."

"He speaks like a woman, not a Modoc," shouted Bogus Charley, and some of the others chanted, "Kill him!"

"No," objected Scar Face. He stepped forward, his rifle in his hand. "What purpose would it serve? Better that we separate. Those who would follow Captain Jack step to his side. Those who believe as Black Jim and Bogus, follow them."

Events were moving so rapidly that Billy could hardly keep up with them. What had happened to his people? What change had come over them since this morning when they left to fight the Warm Springs? All about him was confusion. Warriors who were once friends were arguing in little groups. Women were hurrying to gather their pitifully few belongings to follow their men, no matter what side they chose.

Before long they had sorted themselves out. Beside Captain Jack and his family stood Schonchin John, with his wives and children. Rabbit Ear Dave, too, had allied himself with the chief, as well as four or five more families.

The others had chosen to follow Black Jim. Billy stared at the larger party. Outside of Schonchin John, who had cried angrily that a Modoc must be true to his elected leader, it included all the warriors who had gained the greatest fame as fighting men, Dave Rock, Steamboat Frank, Curly Headed Jack, Shacknasty Jim, Hooker Jim, Mose Kist, Boston Charley, Boncho, Slolux and many others. Even Weium was with them, as well as Curly Headed Doctor. It was a frightening thing to see.

Suddenly he remembered Scar Face Charley. The man Billy admired the most, the man who had been kindest to him, was slow gathering together the members of his family. Now they were assembled, and without looking back Scar Face struck out after Black Jim's company.

Chapter Fourteen

THIS TIME CAPTAIN JACK LED HIS FOLLOWERS OUT OF the lava beds and to the east.

"We must travel fast," he told them, "and leave no tracks."

So Rabbit Ear Dave and one of the other men brought up the rear, doing what they could to conceal the trail. It was not so difficult as Billy had supposed, for each person stepped in the footprint of the one who had gone before, and they were careful not to bend branches on either side. Only an experienced tracker could have found a telltale mark.

On the second day they were halfway to the summit of a wooded mountain. Here the chief ordered that a temporary camp be made. It was a good place, with running water from a mountain stream, and the women said that plenty of kosh and epaws could be found nearby and dug. Some of the men went out and brought back an antelope within the hour, and that night for the first time in many days their stomachs were filled.

Both Captain Jack and Schonchin John agreed that it would be best to waste none of their precious ammunition, so the hunting was by bow. Billy was proud when his arrow brought down a deer, and the chief appointed him one of the regular hunters. Without Curly Headed Doctor to remind them, everyone seemed to have forgotten that he was still a boy without power.

Even Pete Schonchin gave him equal friendship. Billy spent much time with Pete, but on at least two occasions he was able to talk with Captain Jack himself.

"Do you think they will find us?" he was daring enough to ask on one of these occasions.

"They will find us." The chief nodded soberly. "The eyes of the Warm Spring scouts are keen. But our own scouts have keen eyes too. They will give the alarm, and again we will run away."

"And if we are followed?"

"There will be a battle, and this time we will lose," Jack told him calmly. "We are too few in numbers, but at least we can die fighting. It is a better way to end a life than dangling from the white man's rope. I would not like to die that way."

But for a while there was no sign that they had been followed. It was a peaceful time. The sun had grown warm, so the temporary wickiups thrown up by the women were sufficient protection from any night wind. The air was clean and fresh, scented with pine and juniper, and there was no shortage of fresh meat. Sometimes Billy wished things could go on like this forever.

He had even greater hopes that they could continue because now they were being joined by other Modocs. Long Jim and his ancient father arrived in camp one day. Although they had followed Black Jim when the tribe divided, they had broken off. By themselves they had traveled to Yainax before swinging back south. They had come upon Captain Jack's camp by accident, but once there they remained.

There were others, too. Har-kar-gar-ush, whom the white men called Ben Lawyer, and ten warriors with their families had also deserted Black Jim. They had gone south, as far as Clear Lake, but it was difficult to avoid the whites so they came north again. Now they rejoined their former chief, who welcomed them warmly. The addition of ten fighting men would prove useful, although many of their party were very old or very young, and they would be a burden. They also brought disquieting news.

Four of the Modocs, men whom everybody trusted, had surrendered to the enemy to insure their own safety. Bogus Charley, Shacknasty Jim, Hooker Jim, and worst of all, Scar Face Charley, had sold themselves to the white men. In exchange for security for themselves and their families, they had pledged to help track down their own people.

Captain Jack's face grew hard as obsidian when he heard this, and his eyes narrowed so in anger they were like two cracks in the brown stone.

"I will never speak his name again," he declared, and everyone knew whom he meant. Scar Face Charley had been one of the chief's closest friends.

But now Billy understood why Scar Face had followed Black Jim instead of Captain Jack. At the time when the tribe was splitting, Scar Face had spoken for surrender, and he must have decided even then to follow such a course. Knowing that Black Jim could not hold his men together, he had followed him. It made his plans to surrender easier.

One day when the sun was overhead, a guard on picket duty reported that two men on horseback were approaching from the southwest.

Captain Jack, his rifle close beside him, sat on the ground before his wickiup waiting to receive the visitors, while Schonchin John and the other warriors hid themselves nearby. There was no way of knowing whether the horsemen were friends or enemy scouts, but the Modocs were prepared for either. Billy's place among the warriors was not questioned today. He was given bullets for his rifle and told to join the warriors in the underbrush.

Soon the two riders came out into the open and pulled up their horses before the camp. They were Bogus and Scar Face Charley.

Peering at them through the bushes, Billy felt a great surge of hope. Perhaps, like Long Jim and Ben Lawyer, they had undergone a change of heart. Perhaps they had broken with the white men and had come to offer their services to their former chief. Then he saw that they were riding cavalry horses and the rifles in their hands were new and shining, and hope died to be replaced by loathing.

"Why have you come here?" He could hear the voice of Captain Jack speaking from his place before the wickiup. "Do you want to talk to me or fight? I will do either. I know you have sold yourselves to the white soldiers, so do not try to fill my ears with lies."

Schonchin John signaled his warriors, and they came from concealment to line up on either side of

Captain Jack. Their rifles were in their hands and plainly visible. They watched impassively as Scar Face Charley and Bogus dismounted, secured their horses and transfered their rifles to their left hands. But as they approached, right hands extended in friendship, no hand came out to meet them.

Bogus Charley laughed a little nervously.

"This is not a friendly way to greet two of your own people," he said. "Am I a stranger? A dog? No, I am a Modoc and your friend. You should be glad that Scar Face Charley and I did not leave this work to the soldiers. Whenever the soldiers find you, they will shoot you down. But if you return with us, you will be safe. Do battle no more. Go with us to the soldiers' camp. You will find justice there, as we have found justice. I gave myself up some time ago, also all the others. It is a good thing. Now our stomachs are no longer hungry. We get all we want to eat and—"

"Bogus, say no more!" Captain Jack jumped to his feet and his eyes moved contemptuously up and down the two men before him. "You have said enough. You say that you seek me as a friend, but I do not believe you. You and your companion"—he pointed at Scar Face Charley, and the loathing on his face was for all to read—"are not my friends. You are working for the soldiers. You and your companion hope to run me to earth as the fox runs down the rabbit. This you will never do. I will die by my own hand before I let you have the glory of running me to earth."

He would have said more, but he was interrupted by the arrival of three women who had been out digging epaws. Now they screamed that the soldiers were right behind them. Scarcely had they given the alarm when a volley of shots poured into their midst. There

144

were soldiers on the ridge above them, shooting down on the camp.

Immediately all was confusion. Long ago, Scar Face Charley had told Billy what to do in case of such attack. He must take care of himself, run for shelter. He acted on that advice now, and from his place at the end of the line of warriors he scurried for the thicket behind them. Gaining that, he looked back and in that instant saw that Schonchin John was on the ground with Bogus on his back, holding him there. Billy did not wait to see more. The thicket would not serve as a permanent hiding place, and he began pushing his way through and into the pine forest beyond.

How long he ran he wasn't sure, but his breath was labored when he finally stopped. He had left the sounds of rifle fire well behind him, and now all he could hear was the voice of a bird calling from a tree-top and the occasional thud of a pinecone as it fell to the ground.

After a while he got up and started on up the mountain. The land was strange to him, but he kept climbing. He wondered about the other Modocs and how many had been killed in that barrage of bullets. He thought about his mother and Chipmunk, his grandfather and his stepfather and of Captain Jack. Were they still alive? He had no way of knowing.

It was very still on the mountaintop. Because of the trees he could not see the valley below. Somehow it did not seem so safe as it had before. There were wild animals here, bear and wolves, coyotes and cougars. He sat down to rest again and counted his bullets. He had been given only five.

As the blue sky took on a pink glow from the setting sun, he knew he would have to find a place to spend the night. It wasn't easy, but at last he settled on a small hollow where the rising ground at his back would give him some protection. He checked the load in his rifle and sat down, his tired legs stretched out before him. His stomach twitched with hunger and his mouth was dry, but he had seen no mountain stream during the ascent. Perhaps it was just as well, he told himself as darkness settled. His thirst would keep him awake and on guard.

But it didn't. He came to with a start and discovered it was morning. His legs, which had been tired last night, still ached. Every muscle throbbed. Moreover, he was cold. The mountaintop had none of the protection of the camp.

He stood up and stomped his bare feet against the pine needles on the ground, willing the pain to go away. He knew he must have food and water. And perhaps there were others, like himself, who had escaped. He must find them.

The descent was easier than the climb. The sound of running water told him of a stream, and when he found it he had a long drink, dipping his cupped hand and carrying water to his mouth. That was one of the lessons he had learned in that long ago time when he was preparing for his quest. Only a white man throws himself on the ground to drink from the stream itself.

He saw tracks beside the stream where deer had come this way, but there was no sign of the animals themselves. Even if he saw one, Billy reminded himself that he must not waste a precious bullet. His bow and mink quiver filled with arrows had been left behind in the camp. But perhaps, when he found his friends, they would have food.

As he neared the bottom he could see that the path

he had taken was not the same as his ascent. It did not come out at the Modoc's former camp, but led into a valley, a valley he did not recognize. Running toward him through the tall grass was a man he would have known anywhere, a man in a ragged tunic taken from a soldier, with a scarlet band holding his black hair.

"Captain Jack!"

Billy started forward before he realized that the chief was being pursued by a small detatchment of army soldiers led by an Indian scout.

Jack saw him and tried to cry out, but no words were left within him.

Billy turned and would have dashed back the way he had come, but it was too late. Another cavalry unit was approaching along the trail that circled the mountain. One of the soldiers raised his rifle and fired a warning shot in the air.

He stood where he was, and as Jack reached his side the chief threw himself on the ground, panting heavily. Just before the two detachments, one led by Hooker Jim, the other by Scar Face Charley, reached them, he looked up and managed a few words.

"Jack's legs are all worn out," he said.

Chapter Fifteen

BILLY STOOD AT THE WALL OF THE GUARDHOUSE AND peered out through a tiny crack he had discovered between two logs. It was a small crack, but he had made it as large as he dared by chipping at it with a piece of stone. It gave a limited view of Fort Klamath where they were confined.

All of the members of the tribe were here. Billy had been surprised to find Black Jim's followers at Fairchild's ranch when he and Captain Jack arrived. The majority of them were resigned to returning to Fort Klamath. They were tired of fighting, exhausted from running, and they were grateful for their first full meals in weeks. Except for Jim himself and Curly Headed Doctor, they had given in peacefully, and they seemed to hold no grudge against Scar Face Charley, who had served as tracker for the military who brought them in.

It had been six of the white man's weeks since they had been brought here in wagons drawn by four or six mules. The trip had taken ten days and was not without incident. Once, when one of the wagons lagged behind, it was attacked by angry settlers who shot blindly into the ranks of Indians crowded in the back. Five Modocs were killed and several wounded, including Deaf Tom who got a bullet in his arm. Sally, Chipmunk and Rabbit Ear Dave had come through safely.

Another day was made eventful when Curly Headed Jack managed to get hold of a revolver and took his own life. He had been telling everyone that he preferred death to being a prisoner of the whites, but nobody believed he meant it. The wagons had waited while a grave was dug, and Curly Headed Jack was buried beside the road.

Black Jim and Curly Headed Doctor had made the trip with heavy chains binding them together. The soldiers said that they were troublemakers and kept trying to run away. Billy could believe it. He had no love for either Black Jim or Curly Headed Doctor and was indifferent to the chains encircling their ankles, but he was resentful that Captain Jack and Schonchin John had suffered the same indignity.

Now, as he stood at the wall, he wished he could see more of the fort through his tiny chink. Straight ahead and across the square was the building where the trial was going on. There were armed guards standing at the door, and one by one he had watched the Modocs as they were led in to tell their stories of the killings in the Wa Wa Tent. Billy had been called in turn and had answered all the questions of the stern-faced officers sitting around the long table as honestly as he could, but everything he knew had been told to him by Ellen's Man. Now they were calling the women, who were confined separately in the open stockade. He watched carefully, hoping for a glimpse of his mother.

He watched One Eyed Dixie as she was led from the building to be replaced by Betsy Pokumkus. Neither of them would be able to tell the officers what they wanted to know. No women had been in the Wa Wa Tent. But the same could be said for himself, he realized fairly. All the men around the table wanted to know was about that killing. They were not interested in the war or why it had come about. But their interrogations had been thorough. As a result, Boncho and Slolux, who had hidden with rifles outside the Wa Wa Tent, were taken into custody. For some unexplained reason, Bogus and his colleagues had failed to mention them before.

The burly figure of Bogus Charley himself strutted across the square directly into Billy's line of vision. Bogus was wearing new army clothes and had been put in charge of the four deserting Modocs who had served the army as scouts. None of them was confined in the guardhouse, although Bogus, Hooker and Shacknasty Jim visited there sometimes, boasting about their great powers as trackers and their friendship with the soldiers.

Scar Face Charley had come only once, asking to speak with Captain Jack. When the chief refused to see him, Scar Face had turned to the others, and his voice was that of one who asked their understanding.

"I did not know it would come to this," he said. "Our chief has always asked for peace, and I thought that I might help to bring it about. If I had known—"

150

He turned away without saying more.

After that, tribesmen returning from their turn at the trial always reported seeing Scar Face sitting by himself against a wall, his face lined with grief.

Billy turned away from the little chink in the logs, unwilling to look longer at Bogus Charley.

The main room where he was standing was large, but to the Modocs confined there it was almost unbearable. When they looked to the side they saw only walls of wood, and instead of the open sky above there was more wood. It was stifling hot, partly from the summer sun and partly from the heat of their own bodies. They longed for the scent of fresh air.

Along one wall was a series of heavy doors, each leading to a cell. And here, safely secured with metal locks, were those whom the whites considered the chief perpetrators of the crime, Captain Jack, Schonchin John, Boston Charley, Black Jim, Boncho and Slolux. Bogus Charley and Hooker Jim had also participated in the killings in the Wa Wa Tent, thought Billy, but the white man chose to forget about that.

The Modocs thought they had killed Old Man Meacham, but one day he appeared in the guardhouse, thin and pale, with the scars of Schonchin John's knife along his head where an effort had been made to take his scalp. At first everyone thought he was a ghost, but when Curly Headed Doctor, saying special words with every step, advanced to feel the arm beneath the blue coatsleeve, reported it was real, everyone breathed more freely.

Colonel Meacham was going to speak for the Modoc prisoners at their trial, he told them. No one else was willing to do it, so he had volunteered. Every man was entitled to a defense lawyer. He promised to do the best he could.

After he had gone, some of the tribesmen wondered if Old Man Meacham would speak true, or would his words only tighten the ropes about the prisoners' necks? Billy thought the colonel could be trusted. There were good white men as well as bad, just as there were evil Modocs among the good.

There was a rumbling sound of wheels outside, followed by the grating of a key against the lock. As the door swung open, letting in a blaze of dazzling sunlight and a welcome wave of outer air, a two-wheeled cart was rolled inside. Walking behind, but heavily guarded by armed soldiers, was a white man with an enormous growth of whiskers on his face and a shining head upon which grew no hair at all. This always made the Modocs laugh, and because he knew they were laughing at him, the face above the bristling beard never failed to grow red, a flush which extended to the place where the hair line ought to be. That delighted the Indians even more.

Billy had seen many bald-headed men, so he was more interested in the small figure that always trailed this man, who was the cook. Bud was beginning to look better. Regular meals, plus frequent snacks between, were filling out his thin frame and erasing some of the old-man look about his face. His small eyes always darted around the circle of Indians until he found his friend. Then he grinned, and during the business of laying out their meal and delivering dishes and cups to the men inside the locked cells, he always found an opportunity to whisper a few words and slip some extra tidbit into Billy's hand.

Billy moved over against the wall next to the cells to make things easier.

"I fixed it," Bud whispered as he waited for the guard to unlock the cell door. "It's today."

There was no chance for him to say more, and Billy had no idea what he meant. The few sentences that Bud had managed to convey before had been about getting his friend out of the guardhouse. When he thought about it, Billy wasn't sure he wanted to get out. What would he do? He wouldn't want to join the swaggering Bogus or his friends. And like Captain Jack, Billy had turned his back on his one-time friend, Scar Face Charley. Perhaps it was better to stay where he was.

After the guards had escorted the cook cart back outside, he opened his hand to inspect Bud's daily gift. Two pieces of hardtack were all he had been able to manage. Billy gave them both to Pete Schonchin.

Late in the afternoon the outer door was opened again to admit a soldier carrying a rifle.

"Billy Morrison," he called sharply.

At first no one answered, then Rabbit Ear Dave pushed Billy forward.

"You Billy Morrison?" demanded the soldier suspiciously.

"I used to be." His use of the English language made the soldier stare with surprise. "Now I am called Billy Modoc."

"Reckon you must be the one," decided the soldier. "Outside with you."

This must be what Bud meant, thought Billy, as the man marched him across the square and up the single step of a small building. It had something of the appearance of a white man's house. Linkville was filled with houses like it, only they didn't have soldiers with rifles at the entrance.

The guard knocked on the door, and when some-one inside called "Enter," he threw it open.

"The prisoner, Billy Morrison, sir," he announced and pushed the boy through the opening.

If the remainder of the house was a residence, the front room was used as an office. A soldier with gold braid on his uniform was sitting behind a desk. He said nothing, but his visitor, whose back was to the door jumped to his feet.

He turned around, and it was Pa.

"Billy," he roared, but the next moment his face seemed to sag a little. "What they done to you, boy? You look just like a Injun."

"He is an Indian," said the officer. "At least, he's half."

"But the other half's white. As white as you are." Pa spun around to glare at the man, and his eyebrows dropped low over his eyes in the way Billy remembered so well. "All he needs is a haircut and some new duds, and maybe a bit of a scrub. Then you could see how white he is."

"Is this man your father?" The officer looked at Billy, and the boy nodded mutely. His mind was churning so rapidly that he could not find words to speak. So this was the surprise Bud had promised. This was the way he had fixed things up!

"How old are you?" asked the officer.

"He's only thirteen," said Pa promptly, and Billy let it go although he knew he was nearing his fifteenth birthday.

"And you've lived with the Modocs two years?"

"It was two years come March since he lit out to

154

find his ma. You see, I took me a new wife after she left. A white woman," explained Pa. "And I reckon the boy was a mite put out. He'd had me all to hisself before, you understand. He was always a good boy, Billy was. Quiet and hard working, a real help in my livery stable."

The officer picked up some papers from his desk, and his eyes studied the writing.

"This is a transcript of his testimony from the trial," he explained. "I see that he took part in only two encounters with the army. The last was when the Modoc camp was surrounded and no shot was fired by the Indians. The other was the massacre at Black Ledge when the unit headed by Captain Thomas was ambushed. The boy admits that at that time he did not use his rifle. Apparently he had no ammunition."

And because I didn't know how, thought Billy silently. Scar Face hadn't taught me yet. He wished he hadn't been quite so honest when they asked him all those questions. He felt like a baby standing there, a baby without words, though the sight of Pa had brought back memories that he thought he had buried forever.

"If I release him in your custody you will be responsible for him, Mr. Morrison. Can you guarantee his good behavior?" The white man leaned forward over the desk. "Otherwise, he will be sent to Quawpaw Agency in Indian Territory. It might be the best thing for the boy. Oklahoma is a long way. People there have never heard of the Modocs. In Oregon and California, feelings run very high. I cannot answer for his safety if he stays here."

"I can," promised Pa confidently. "Nobody around

Linkville's likely to stand up to me. And Billy will behave hisself. He knows I'll wallop the tar out of him if he don't."

"Very well." The officer leaned back, and after dipping his pen in the inkstand, began making marks on a paper on his desk. "You may take him with you, Mr. Morrison. And remember, the responsibility is yours."

"Thank you, sir." Pa turned and slapped Billy on the back. "I got a couple of saddle horses outside. Come along, son. We're going home."

Chapter Sixteen

PA'S HOUSE LOOKED DIFFERENT. AS THEY RODE INTO the yard through the gathering dusk, Billy could see that another room had been added on, and there was the flutter of curtains at an open window. Tidy flower beds had been planted on either side of the front step, and he caught the fragrance of some blossom he did not know.

It had been a silent ride from the fort, although in the beginning Pa tried to make conversation. Most of it was about the residents of Linkville. McVey had retired and now Pa was the sheriff, with a deputy to help him. He had George Hooper working at the livery stable, but now that Billy was back he would let George go. The man was half-witted anyway. Etta had become practically the sole dictator of all women's groups in the church. Nobody made a suggestion or decision without consulting her. The new baby had been a daughter. Pa referred to her as Lila, said she was about two, and that Etta claimed she was very smart for her age. The town was growing so fast Billy would hardly know it. Some of the citizens had volunteered for service in the beginning of the Modoc war, but most of them had come back early. It was a matter for the soldiers to take care of, anyway, since they were being paid for it.

When he discovered that his son made no comment on any subject he brought up, Pa finally stopped talking altogether, and Billy was relieved.

He hadn't wanted to return to Linkville, and he was angry with Bud for sending for Pa. But no one had asked his preference, and now that he thought of it he wasn't too sure he wanted to stay with the Modocs either.

Billy had heard tales about reservations, and they hadn't been pleasant. Thin blankets, weevily flour, white man's tough beef brought in twice a month and doled out to each family with instructions to make it last. The Modocs' guns had already been confiscated, and Rabbit Ear Dave said it was unlikely they would be given back. Probably their ponies wouldn't be returned either. The strange place where they were being taken was so far away. Someone said two mountain chains must be crossed to get there, and even then it was some distance beyond. The people were fearful of this land ahead of them, and even more so of the way they must reach it. Wagons would transport them to a town called Redding, and then they would be loaded onto a huge, noisy monster made of iron that moved without the aid of horses and breathed quantities of evil-smelling smoke. Even Curly Headed Doctor admitted he had no power as great as this magic.

"Well, come along, Billy," ordered Pa, throwing his leg over the saddle. "We're home. Bet it feels good to get here."

Billy slid to the ground and stood waiting uncertainly. Pa grabbed his arm and ushered him up the step. He seemed to hesitate a moment before opening the door, then he boldly lifted the latch and threw it back.

"Well, here we are!" he shouted. "Hungry enough to eat them two horses outside."

At his urging Billy stepped forward. The room no longer looked familiar. There was a braided rug on the floor and an iron cookstove in the corner. The bed against the wall was covered by a pieced quilt of many colors. He had no time to see more for there was a startled scream from the rocker beside the fire.

"A wild Injun! Moses Morrison, you get that wild Injun out of here! You hear?"

Mrs. Etta stood up, her thin face white with terror. She must have been rocking the small child in her arms, and now she clutched it tightly to her breast.

"Pshaw, Etta," protested Pa. "This ain't no wild Injun. It's only Billy. I fetched him home."

"You did what?" Angry spots of red blossomed suddenly on the still, white face, and the child in her arms began to cry. "Now look what you did," the mother accused. "You scared little Delilah. Get that savage out of my house right away."

"It's my house, too," insisted Pa stubbornly. "I tell you this ain't no wild Injun. It's just Billy. He's my son, and the only one I'm likely to ever have at that."

Billy didn't know what made him do it. Maybe it was because Mrs. Etta kept retreating farther and farther away from him, but all of a sudden he opened his mouth and out came a perfect Modoc war whoop.

Mrs. Etta screamed again, her back now firmly pressed against the wall, and the little girl cried louder. She looked so funny in her terror that even Pa must have noticed it for his rebuke was mild.

"Now, Billy, you stop that. What you want to scare your ma and your little sister for, anyhow?"

"Squaw not Billy's ma." Encouraged by Pa's reception to his outburst, Billy spoke in an imitation of Scar Face Charley's stilted English. "Papoose not Billy's sister. Me wild Injun. Modoc eat him both for breakfast."

"Moses!" shrieked Mrs. Etta.

"I had enough of this from both of you," shouted Pa. This time Billy had gone too far. "Etta, you stop yelling like that and get us some supper. Billy, you stop acting that way or I'll rip your hide wide open. Now set down and wait for your vittles."

Billy sat down in one of the straight chairs at the table. He was surprised at his own behavior and equally surprised at Pa's reception of it. He must be mistaken, but it almost seemed that Pa had enjoyed his wife's discomfort.

He looked at his little half-sister, Delilah, who was still crying and clinging to her mother's long skirts as Mrs. Etta began putting supper on the table. As he had always imagined, the child was far inferior to Chipmunk. Her skin was very white and the reddish-blonde hair that had been braided in two short pigtails looked thin and fine. Her face was distorted from crying, but he could tell that she was going to resemble her mother.

"You only put on two plates," observed Pa. "You

and Lila et already?"

"Yes—no, we're not hungry." Mrs. Etta's mouth bit at the words viciously.

"Suit yourself," said Pa, pulling up a chair and cutting a huge slice from the roast. "Help yourself, Billy."

The food was good, better than he had been given at Fort Klamath. After the roast and vegetables, there was berry pie, and at Pa's urging Billy ate two pieces.

"Where's he going to sleep?" asked Mrs. Etta. She had gone back to the rocking chair and taken the little girl onto her lap again. "At the stable, same as before?"

"No," said Pa. "I been giving that some thought. Until the town gets used to him again, Billy'd better stick close to me. Like you say, he does resemble a Injun some, and the way folks feel it might not be a good idea to send him off alone. He'll sleep with me."

"Then see to it that he has a bath before he gets under my clean quilts," she ordered shortly.

Pa, it seemed, had built the addition to the house for his own use. He told Billy that he had slept there since his daughter was born. Mrs. Etta said it would be better for them both. She wouldn't wake him when she got up at night to tend the baby, and besides he snored. She hadn't had a full night's sleep since they were married, and she didn't want to develop vapors.

The room was small. It only accommodated a bed, but it had a fireplace. Pa managed to squeeze in a washtub, filled it with water and handed Billy a cake of homemade soap and a towel.

"You need it," he said frankly. "You stink like a buffalo skinner."

161

Billy knew that he was right. There had been no sanitary facilities, no place to wash themselves, in the guardhouse where the Modocs were confined. He washed as thoroughly as he could and wished that he had other clothes to wear.

But Pa had thought of that, too. He gave his son a pair of his own pants and a clean shirt. The pants were too large around and he had to hold them up with a rope, but in length they fitted perfectly.

"Etta will be glad to wash your old ones for you," he declared. "And first thing tomorrow we'll see about cutting your hair."

This trip to Mr. Barnes's barber shop was very different from the other times. In the first place, Mr. Barnes didn't recognize him, and even when he was convinced that it was really Billy, he was reluctant to cut his hair.

"I don't cotton to no Injun," he declared.

"Billy ain't no Injun. He's my own son," insisted Pa angrily. "Now you give him your best haircut, Pete, providing you don't want trouble with me. And cut it short."

Sulkily, the barber motioned to Billy to take the barber chair.

Billy felt real pain as he saw the black strands fall to the floor. It had taken a long time to grow his hair to this length. There was a different kind of pain, too, for more than once the barber nicked him with the scissors.

Finally he could stand it no longer, and since a dog fight down the street had caused Pa to step momentarily outside, he spoke to Mr. Barnes about it.

"You cut Billy one more time," he declared, "me take scissors. Use them to scalp you with."

162

The barber shuddered slightly. He made no reply, but there were no more nicks.

When they left, Pa led the way to Quincy's General Store. Here they purchased shoes, a new plaid shirt and a pair of heavy cotton pants.

"Don't suppose you want underwear," said Mr. Quincy, when Pa had finished his selection. There was an insulting sneer to his voice, enough to make Pa glower. Billy knew that he hadn't thought of underwear. It was summer, and underwear went on at the beginning of winter. But now Pa was determined to have some.

"'Course we want underwear," he declared. "What you figure my son to be? Some kind of heathen that runs around without underbritches?"

With the new clothes over Billy's arm and the stiff new shoes on his calloused feet, they finally reached the livery stable. Here everything was as he remembered it. Nothing was changed. Well, almost nothing. George Hooper hadn't been here before.

Pa hadn't been far wrong when he accused George Hooper of being half-witted. He was of middle age, but he still had the unlined face of a boy. He was small and wiry, and as they entered he stared at Billy with open curiosity.

"That your boy, Mr. Morrison? The one that's part Modoc?"

"How'd you know about that?" Billy knew that Pa's patience had been strained to the breaking point.

"Oh, the whole town's talking." George must be impervious to Pa's fits of temper, for he continued to stare. "They said if you brung him back, they'll ride him right out again on a rail. Maybe with tar and feathers on him, too. But he don't look so fierce to me.

Hardly looks like a Injun. They always have long hair and he don't have as much as I got." He smiled at Billy happily, and Billy smiled back.

"They better not try nothing," threatened Pa. "And I'll tell them so. Don't you worry, Billy."

"I'm not worried." Surprisingly, he wasn't.

"Tell you what, though," decided Pa slowly. "You better stay on a spell, George. Won't hurt to have two of you here. And if there looks like there's going to be any trouble, any trouble at all, you hightail it down to the sheriff's office after me. Hear that, George?"

If there had been plans underfoot to rid the town of Billy, they didn't materialize. But his life was anything but pleasant, and he knew that Pa's wasn't either.

Mrs. Etta never spoke to him. She refused to wash his clothes, and while she allowed him to eat at the table neither she nor Lila ever sat down with him or Pa. Billy had grown accustomed to Modoc women waiting until their men had finished eating before they themselves ate, but Pa never gave up urging her to join them.

The days when Billy had to move off the sidewalk to make way for the whites were gone. It was they who moved aside, but the looks they gave him were filled with hatred. He told himself he didn't care, but it was hard to live in a place where everyone disliked you. Sometimes he wondered if it would be better if he ran away again. That place across two mountain chains might be better than living here. Then he remembered that if he went to the reservation he would be a prisoner. Here, at least, he was free.

But was it enough to be free? Every day he must suffer the resentment and dislike of the townspeople.

164

They did not want him here. They endured him only because they were afraid of Pa, and perhaps of Billy himself. It was hard to live in a place where he could not count a single friend, except perhaps for George, who was half-witted, and Pa, who was determined that people must accept his son. Sometimes he wondered if there was a place for him anywhere.

Neither he nor George had enough to occupy their time in the livery stable, for business fell off. Townspeople gave up renting teams or buggies, and new barns to stable horses at home were rising in many backyards. Pa never mentioned it, but one night he talked about something else.

After they finished supper they went to the new room, and since there wasn't space for a chair they both sat on the edge of the bed.

"Billy, it ain't going to work," began Pa uncomfortably. "I done my best. I wanted it to work, but I can't fight it no more. Today they said they was going to vote me out of office, not let me be sheriff no more. You know how much that means to me."

Yes, Billy knew. The shining star on his shirt and the hours away from home when he could swagger a little and regain some of his self-respect were all Pa had left. He knew, too, that in his own way Pa loved him, that he had tried to make the town accept his son. He had never felt close to his father before, but he did now.

"I'll go away," he offered cheerfully. "Maybe the reservation won't be so bad."

"Not that," objected his father hastily. "The reservation is for Injuns. You're half white, Billy. You got my blood in you. It's good blood, too, and thick. That's why my brother come to mind."

"Your brother?"

"Oh, I got a brother, all right, though I ain't laid eyes on him for quite a spell. Before you was born, it was. He lives in Frisco."

It was the first time Pa had mentioned having a brother. Why, that would make him Billy's uncle. It was strange to have an uncle he had never heard of.

"He's a preacher," explained Pa, a little apologetically. "He never had much use for me, not after we was growed up. But he'll take to you right off."

"Why should he?"

"Because you're another soul to save," explained Pa earnestly. "And there's nothing Aaron likes better than saving souls. I'm giving you a good saddle horse and fifty dollars. You think you can find the way to Frisco by yourself?"

Billy nodded a little blankly. His head was whirling.

"The weather's holding, so you'll have a month to cross the pass, but you mustn't wait much longer," continued Pa. "First thing tomorrow I want you to light out. I got a letter here for you to give to Aaron, and when he reads it he'll take over. You won't have to worry about nothing from then on."

Chapter Seventeen

A GREAT CROWD WAS POURING INTO THE OPEN GATES of Fort Klamath when Billy arrived there the next morning. There had been many wagons filled with whites, as well as riders on horseback on the road, but now they were being joined by masses of grinning Klamath Indians. Everyone was headed in the same direction that he had taken, and he decided they must be going to attend some kind of festival.

If he had followed Pa's instructions, he would have turned south after leaving Linkville. Instead he went north. There were good-byes to say for which he had been given no time before. His mother, Chipmunk, his old grandfather, Rabbit Ear Dave, Pete Schonchin and Captain Jack all deserved a proper farewell. And, of course, there was Bud, although Billy was still a little angry with Bud for having sent for Pa.

The crowd seemed to be congregating in a

meadow a little beyond the stockade that held the women prisoners. Some of the people were sitting on the ground, others were milling around, talking to their friends.

Billy tied his horse and started toward the stockade. There were gaps between the poles, not wide enough to permit the smallest child to squeeze through, but larger than the chink he had made in the guardhouse. If he could attract the attention of someone inside, he could ask her to call his mother.

As he passed the guardhouse where the men were confined, he noticed that today the number of soldiers on duty was increased. All were dressed in their best uniforms, and their freshly shined brass buttons glittered in the morning sun. Whatever the day's festivities, they included the army as well as civilians.

Billy did not stop, but as he neared the stockade, he saw a curious construction in the meadow around which the visitors were collecting. It was a platform about thirty feet long, which could be mounted by a series of steps. Beams had been erected from either end, with a heavy bar extending between them. From the bar hung six long ropes.

His breath caught in his throat and his knees grew so weak they would hardly hold him up. The thing that Captain Jack had dreaded most of all was about to happen. It was going to happen today, and all those people collected around the gallows were here to enjoy the spectacle.

"*Kwa, kwa, kwa!*"

The sound reached him through the muffled beating of a giant drum—his own heart pounding in his ears.

168

"Billy! I never figured to see you here again."
Bud came running toward him across the grass. "Did
you come to see the hanging?"

"No. I didn't know it was going to happen." He
didn't even glance at the boy, for beyond he could see
three familiar figures, Bogus Charley, Hooker and
Shacknasty Jim. They, too, had shined the buttons on
their coats and now they were strutting proudly toward the crowd.

Two of those ropes should have been for them,
thought Billy bitterly. Both Bogus Charley and Hooker
Jim had taken part in the murders in the Wa Wa Tent.
Was it white man's justice that they were allowed to
go free while the others were punished?

"Then why did you come?" Bud's thin hand
plucked at his sleeve.

"I came to say good-bye." He answered almost
automatically while his eyes skimmed the outer bound-
aries of the fort.

In the farthest corner was a humped-over mass of
blue. Scar Face Charley was sitting alone in his favorite spot, but today he had turned his back so he
would not have to face the gallows. For the first time
since the tribe divided, Billy felt a little sorry for the
man who had been so good to him. Whether or not
Scar Face was telling the truth and really believed
that the crime committed in the Wa Wa Tent would
be forgiven, the consequences of his own betrayal were
something he would have to live with all his life.

"To me?" Bud's pleasure was evident in his voice.
"I'm glad you didn't go away without saying good-bye
to me, Billy. You're still the best friend I ever had. My
only friend, really. I don't want you to go away. I'll

even go back to Linkville if you'll stay there, too. I hate it around here, anyway. You don't know what it's been like."

Billy looked at the boy beside him. There was affection, real affection in those small eyes that looked up into his. Billy had made other friends, Ellen's Man, Scar Face Charley, Pete Schonchin, but none had proved himself so loyal as Bud. Real friendship was not a temporary thing. It endured. It came to him that Bud was as much an outsider as he himself. Bud hadn't fitted into life at Linkville, and apparently the army had been no better. Maybe there wasn't any place in the world for him, either, or maybe the two of them just hadn't found it yet. But at least they could try.

"I'm going to San Francisco," he said quickly. "I've got a letter to my uncle there, if I decide to use it. I've got a horse and fifty dollars. Do you want to come with me?"

"Do I?" The thin face shone with eagerness, and Bud jiggled with excitement. "When can we leave?"

"When is *it* going to happen?" Billy nodded toward the six ropes swinging from the cross bar.

"Ten o'clock," Bud told him promptly. "In about an hour."

"Let me say good-bye to my mother first. She can tell the others," said Billy. It would have to be a short leave-taking. He didn't want to be here when the prisoners were led from the guardhouse. "Then we'll go. I don't know what's going to happen, Bud, but we'll be together. There'll be two of us."

Author's Note

ON THE MORNING OF OCTOBER 3, 1873, CAPTAIN JACK, Schonchin John, Black Jim and Boston Charley were executed for the murders of General Canby and the Reverend Mr. Thomas. At the eleventh hour, the sentences of Boncho and Slolux were changed to life imprisonment at the Federal penitentiary on Alcatraz Island.

Close to a million dollars of government money had been poured into the campaign against the Modocs, and the number of Americans killed almost equaled those lost in battles during the Spanish American war.

Members of the Modoc tribe were shipped by railroad cars to Quawpaw Agency, Indian Territory, Oklahoma. In 1909, the survivors and their descendants were returned and restored to the rolls of the Klamath Agency in Oregon. Even after all those years, their arrival was not heralded with joy by the Klamath tribe or most of the residents of Linkville, which in the interim had become the city of Klamath Falls.

Today the lava beds have become a National Monument. Visitors may see carefully marked battle-grounds, encircled by a well-kept road, descend underground into artificially lighted caves and explore Captain Jack's Stronghold where for six months some fifty Modocs held off a thousand Federal and volunteer fighting men.

The Indians in this book are real, as are the U.S. Army officers, the negotiators and the events which took place on the battlefield. Only Billy and the white settlers in Linkville, while typical of the era, are fictitious.

The fact that there are a number of Charleys, Jacks, Jims, etc. among Modoc names is sometimes confusing and must be blamed upon the whites who conferred them. White men's names, like white men's clothing, were greatly prized by the Modocs and Klamaths. They did not feel justified in taking a name for themselves and good-natured white men gave them carelessly.

Many histories have been written about the Modoc War of 1872–73, but the one on which I relied the most was *The Indian History of the Modoc War* by Jeff C. Riddle, first printed in 1914 and reprinted in 1974 by the Urion Press, Eugene, Oregon. Mr. Riddle was the son of Tobey and Frank Riddle, and while he was only ten years old at the time of the battles, he knew personally all the Indians who took part and later listened to their stories.

Tobey was later renamed Winema by the whites, and under that name her memory is kept alive in the area as the heroine that she was.